# To Die and Live

By Steven J. Losee

Writers Exchange E-Publishing

http://www.writers-exchange.com

To Die and Live: A Bill Donley Novel
Copyright 2008, 2015, 2023 Steven J. Losee
Writers Exchange E-Publishing
PO Box 372
ATHERTON QLD 4883

Cover Art by Odile Stamanne

Published by Writers Exchange E-Publishing
http://www.writers-exchange.com

# Part 1:

## SMUGGLER'S RANSOM

# Chapter 1

## October, 1984

I never learned the nature of the super-secret information that leaked out of the United States from Cape Canaveral and Houston Control, but it wasn't necessary for me to know that. I did learn that it would travel through Mexico and Central America, across to Cuba and then all the way to the Kremlin. Someone with authority finally got angry and frustrated enough about the leakage to launch an operation to plug it.

Covert investigation teams worked around the clock in Florida and Texas until somebody found the group's stateside base, or "safe house", in Houston.

I'd never know who found it, but it didn't matter. That wasn't my job.

My job was interception and dispatch.

Of course, any self-respecting undercover type could do the intercept. At the very least, those who worked at home should know how to keep information from getting out of the country. It was the "dispatch" part that brought me into it. The official terminology is "counter assassination"--in other words, "waste the bums". That kind of assignment tends to make some people squeamish and reluctant.

Not me, though. That's my job.

The night air was warm, but I didn't mind. I'd just passed three hours in one of those Texas honky-tonks watching "cowboys" doing the two-step to an endless succession of sound-alike songs about lost girls, pickup trucks, dogs and dead horses. I shouldn't judge, though. I can barely remember the words to "Happy Birthday". We won't even discuss what I do to the melody.

I sauntered up the street a few steps behind a noisy bar hopping group of four: three guys and one girl. As they passed the house in question, I slipped up to the door and had it open in ten seconds. Once in, I checked all the nooks and crannies, just to make sure no one else was there.

The living room was hardly furnished at all. No pictures on the walls, no couch, no easy chairs. Just a few folding chairs and two folding tables. One table was against the far wall with only a telephone on it.

I made note of the computer terminal on the other table in the middle of the room. The disc being delivered would no doubt be inspected before payment was made. Then I went to the telephone and fished in my pockets until I found the gadget. I've never been fond of gadgets. It's too easy to start depending on them. Then one day the batteries run out and you have to rely on your own strength and wits. What a tragedy.

I planted it on the bottom of the phone and pressed a button on my government issue watch.

The shrill ringing of the phone split the silence of the room. I let it ring twice more, just to make sure it was working properly, then pressed the button again to stop the racket.

I smirked at the immediate silence. *My tax dollars at work*, I thought.

My cynicism was cut short by a sound outside. I slipped behind a cabinet and eased the safety off my Glock before the door opened.

I heard the door close, then footsteps, and something being placed on the floor.

After what felt like a long silence, the door opened again. There was some quick shuffling, and then the voices began.

"Let's get this over with," a man said. He was frightened and nervous. Not a professional, this one.

"Oooh, you poor baby," crooned a familiar female voice. Maria Maltevar, code-name Minnie Mouse. I'd almost killed her once. This job was going to be a pleasure. "Does selling your country's secrets make you nervous?"

I almost chuckled. That's something traitors never seem to learn: even the people they sell out to despise them.

He didn't want to hear it. "Aw, shut up! Where's the money?"

Money. The same old, boring story.

I heard something being placed on the table and two clicks: a briefcase of some kind being opened.

"Right here, darling," Maria said. Then the syrup went out of her voice and she snapped, "Now where is the disc?"

I heard the hum as the computer was turned on, the clicking of the keys, and a feminine grunt of interest. I gave her just enough time to get a good look. Then I hit the button on my watch.

The telephone rang on cue and the tension level went up about a thousand percent.

"Who could that be?" Maria snapped, annoyed.

In one fluid motion, I stepped out and aimed. They were both at the computer, faces to the telephone, with their backs to me.

Just for effect I said, "Avon calling!"

Maria whirled around and reached for her own gun.

I gave her just enough time to recognize me before I pulled the trigger. She jerked as a small hole appeared between her eyes and the back of her head blew away.

My American friend was losing control. He went down on all fours in front of me. While he groveled, he groped for Maria's pistol, but his hands wouldn't cooperate. He whimpered like a frightened puppy, and he couldn't take his eyes off what had been Maria Maltevar.

I went into a forward roll as he finally grasped the piece and started to rise. Thoroughly enjoying myself, I came up facing him across the computer terminal. His voice went up an octave as I grinned before putting him out of his misery.

The phone continued ringing as I pulled the disc out of the terminal and counted the money. Five hundred thousand. Cheap at half the price, and not nearly enough. I stuffed everything into the briefcase; Maria's, no doubt; the money was still in it.

In a little while the gang in the Kremlin would know something was wrong and send investigators. Then, when they knew the score, they'd find a way to alert the authorities without revealing themselves. I wanted to be out of town while they were all rummaging around and out of the state while they were looking for me.

I pushed the button on my watch and the incessant ringing stopped.

One more quick look around, and a thorough search through two corpses' pockets, and I was almost ready.

Minnie Mouse and her rat were dead. "Not a creature was stirring..."

I retrieved the gadget from under the phone and slipped it back into one of my pockets.

"Wrong number!" I announced to the room.

Then I slipped out the door, trying to move quickly while blending with the shadows.

# Interlude

Once upon a time in a faraway place, the Pentagon, the Joint Chiefs of Staff held a midnight meeting. The directors of the Central Intelligence Agency and the Federal Bureau of Investigation were there also. All existing intelligence organizations had become too well known for certain kinds of work. Someone else had to be found. So an office was opened in a nondescript building on Pennsylvania Avenue not far from the White House. At the helm was a petite, baby-faced woman, who is only known as...Chase. When the job is too dirty or dangerous for anybody else, they give it to her. Then she gives it to somebody like me.

# *Chapter 2*

The trip to the Houston airport and out of town was routine. I slept on the flight.

As the plane was landing at Dulles International Airport, I had the earphones on, listening to the news. Two people had been fatally shot in a rented house in Houston. It was believed that the house was a place of assignation, or a "love nest". That meant they'd found out the name on the lease was bogus. The man in question had been a junior statesman from Vermont, and his wife was in custody. A manhunt was underway for the woman's husband or whatever. They obviously believed he'd be the perpetrator.

*That's fine*, I thought. *Play up that old angle. No one would ever know why they were really there...except Maria's employers. They weren't about to set the record straight.*

A taxi that had seen better days, with a driver to match, brought me to the building I wanted. I really wanted to go home and pack. Unfortunately, we had strict standing orders to report for debriefing before doing anything else.

The lobby was done in the style that I call "modern corporate". Fake black and white marble floor and walls, with lots of aluminum and glass. Mirrors were a maddeningly large part of the design. But that was so the plainclothes guards could inconspicuously watch people.

On my way across the lobby, I smiled and made secret hand-signals to all the unseen security cameras.

I do that just often enough to keep them off-balance. When they chew me out about it, I excuse myself by calling it a conditioned reflex.

I played it straight on the elevator, composing myself. I didn't want anything to go wrong with this little interview. The elevator let me off and I approached my boss's door.

It was debriefing time.

I gave my usual "shave-and-a-haircut" knock and heard the "Come in" as I turned the knob and stepped into the room.

It was a spartan office - white walls, one window, a couple of degrees and citations, and no pictures. No flowers, frills or decorations. To the left, a little table stood with a decanter and a few glasses on it. The decanter was always filled with some kind of rotgut nobody could stand. I could never figure out why she had it there. She never invited me to have some. Maybe she drank the stuff herself when nobody was watching.

Straight ahead was a plain desk with two gray desk chairs facing it and one high back executive chair behind it.

And Chase, of course. She had her usual subdued, blue outfit...as far as I could see from the other side of the desk. She was looking at me in the pleasantly impersonal way that secretaries and salespeople have turned into an art.

"Ah, Mr. Donley," she said. "Have a seat."

I took the advice without comment and waited.

"I understand the assignment went well."

I nodded. "Dispatch accomplished..." I shot an imaginary gun, "and the classified information is secure." With that, I tossed the little disk onto her desk. It slid until her hand snatched it up.

Chase wasn't into mourning, especially for enemies and traitors. "Excellent! I don't know what we'd do if that information got into the wrong hands."

I resisted the feeble temptation to show interest in the information. She knew what I was waiting to hear. I could sense the stall. I forced the issue. "I don't mean to change the subject, but there's a little matter of three weeks' vacation that I'm scheduled to take."

Her eyes became distant, even though her smile pretended to be reassuring. "And you'll get it, Mr. Donley," she said, "You'll get it."

My mind said, "Here we go again!" but my mouth just said, "I don't think I like the sound of that."

She began to lose her cool. She always did that when she was on my side, but didn't want me to know it. "I'm sorry, Bill, but I have no choice! An emergency has come up. There's no one else available with your clearance level."

It was flattering, of course. That was her way of saying I was the most capable agent available. We all had the same clearance level, but we weren't supposed to know that. However, I was tired, so I started to lose my own cool. I managed to go on without raising my voice. "I'm starting to get sick and tired of your emergencies."

That did it. She swore, banged the desk and said, "So am I, but there's nothing I can do about it!"

I held a hand up. This was no time for a labor dispute. "Okay, forget it. Just tell me. What's this week's emergency?"

She grimaced at the sarcasm before getting down to business. "Do you remember Dr. Emilio Gonsalo?"

I had to think a moment. "Gonsalo?" Then I remembered. "Oh, yeah! He's that Cuban who was trained in Nuclear physics by the Russians. We helped him defect to the United States a couple of years ago, didn't we?"

She nodded. "Yes, with his daughter. Anyway, she went to some church in New York City and became a Born-Againer. Do you know what they are?"

Born-Againer. That phrase triggered a memory. I was very small, playing on the living room floor. My mother was leaning forward in her chair, saying, "Billy!" with a big smile. That was it, like a flashbulb going off, and it was gone. But it left a lingering sadness and yearning I couldn't understand.

Chase made a concerned face at me. "Are you okay?"

I shook my head to clear it. "Oh, sure. I just remembered that my mother was one of them, but she died when I was about twelve. I don't remember much about them, though; just a bunch of religious nuts who aren't allowed to do anything." Intended to be a funny remark, it left me feeling sour and guilty.

She smirked and chuckled. "Not quite, but it's not important. The point is that, because of this experience, she decided she'd...save the communists, or something." Taking a deep breath, she went on, "She joined this group who smuggle Bibles into communist countries..."

"And got caught!" I finished, with triumphant disgust.

"Right."

"I can guess the rest. They found out who she is and are threatening to throw away the key unless we hand over her daddy."

She nodded. "That's it, basically. Her father is hysterical. He's almost considering giving himself up to them for her safety."

I couldn't help snorting. "Sure. They can still throw the key away and blackmail all kinds of work out of him. Did this happen in Cuba?"

"No, she was smart enough to stay out of there. She's in Romania."

I shriveled inside. Not an eastern bloc country; not the Balkans. I hated the Balkans; being there always depressed me. Everything seemed grey: buildings, streets, clothing, people. And I was about to be sent there again.

Instead of my vacation.

I got up and went to the table with my decanter. There was a bottle I hadn't noticed with it, so I picked it up and read the label. It was some obscure kind of rum, over a hundred proof. I looked up and said, "Tiger Sweat?!" as if that was the brand name.

She was in no mood for it. A shrug and a wave was all I got for my humor.

I poured some into a glass anyway and got ready to say my piece. "That's just terrific. Instead of the vacation I was promised, you want me to sneak into Romania, break some religious hippie out of a maximum-security prison and bring her safely back to the land of milk..." I paused for effect and took a healthy swallow. Big mistake. It went down as smoothly as salt water mixed with battery acid. "...and honey!" I spluttered.

Chase looked mildly amused. "Not exactly. They didn't put her in prison. She's under house arrest somewhere. Her comfort is guaranteed until they hear from us." Then she stood up, her sign of dismissal. "So, the sooner you begin, the better all around."

"I can take a hint." I said, and put the glass down.

She was silent until I opened the door to leave. "Excuse me, Mr. Donley?"

I turned. "Yeah?"

She looked puzzled. "You travel all over the world in the line of duty. You go to Hawaii, Puerto Rico, Bermuda, Europe... Tell me something. If...I mean, when you get your vacation, where will you go?"

I shrugged. "I don't know. Brooklyn, I guess."

# *Chapter 3*

My first stop was Paris. I was traveling light, since I didn't expect to be there more than a few hours.

As far as I'm concerned, Paris is better than the Balkans, but not by much. If you're not French, you can get the impression that they'd rather you didn't exist. It was picturesque enough, but seemed fragile and unreal. I sensed an undercurrent of hostility that was probably political, which made it hard to relax.

If I ever got my vacation, I wouldn't take it in Paris.

The taxi let me off at the address I wanted on the Rue De Vaurigard, so I stepped right across the sidewalk and inside. I kept my face forward, though my eyes took in the surrounding area.

The bar was on the right, tables on the left and in back. I walked slowly, letting my eyes adjust to the dim interior.

The only light in the place came from small lamps designed to look like candles. Even the bulbs were shaped like little flames, and they cast just enough light to look at the person across the table. Moreover, the walls were black, with dim gold flake designs here and there.

Middle-aged couples sat at some of the tables, trying to act like they were still in their twenties and could hardly control their gooey-eyed passion. The champagne they all sipped or chug-a-lugged helped them maintain their fantasyland...as long as the light remained this dim.

I ignored all of that as well as I could. The man I was looking for always sat alone. That is, unless he was doing business.

He sat at his usual table, tucked into a corner next to the kitchen door, listening with rapt attention to a young couple. They were animated, interrupting each other and nodding in agreement, though they kept their voices low.

Their talk went on for quite a while. The other patrons were too involved in themselves and each other to notice me. I felt conspicuous anyway. Occupational disease, I guess.

Finally, they were up and heading for the door. I picked up my glass and approached his table, using the name I knew was false. "M. LeChance?"

He'd been musing about something. He turned his eyes to me, and they grew as he recognized me. "Ah, M. Donley! What an unexpected pleasure! Please, have a seat."

I sat and smiled at him. Grey moustache, bald head, blue ageless eyes and old body. I knew he was missing a leg. I'd never seen him away from this table and no one ever talked about his past or description. Therefore, I still didn't know which leg he was missing.

"Now," he said, his smile filled with sincerity, "what can I do for you, eh, mon ami?"

I raised an eyebrow. "What makes you think this isn't just a social call?"

He laughed softly. "So, you wish to climb inside the brain of LeChance, eh? You wish me to explain my reasoning like the English Holmes or the little Belgian, eh? Well, did you know that they were both modeled after the Frenchman, C. Auguste Dupin?"

I shrugged. "That may be, but Dupin was created by an American."

"Touché!"

"As a matter of fact," I went on, "none of those men ever really existed. But you're here and I'm here right now."

"Ah, yes! The here and now are what truly and only interests you. Your imagination is poverty-stricken. No matter. I will explain.

"I do not expect the 'social call' from M. Donley because I know that he does not care for my beloved Paris. He gets off the plane, he comes to LeChance, and he gets on the plane! But always he calls first. Now, suddenly M. Donley is here, but he has not called first. So I think, 'Is Donley fond of LeChance?' Beh! Donley does not know LeChance. He only knows the excellent service he receives from LeChance.

"And now, mon ami, I am back to my first question: what can I do for you?"

I wiped the grin off my face and leaned forward slightly. "Dr. Emilio Gonsalo's daughter is being detained somewhere in Romania until he presents himself to the authorities there."

He sat back and thought, his eyes staring at nothing as he rubbed his chin with his thumb and index finger. Finally, when his memory had sorted things out, he said, "She was abducted?"

I shook my head. "No, she entered the country voluntarily and was discovered."

Now it was his turn to shake his head. "The child was a fool to go to such a place."

"That's what I think," I commented, "but she didn't come to me first."

"Why would she go there?" he said, in sincere confusion.

It wasn't really classified, and I was hoping to get information. I gave it to him. "She was smuggling Bibles in."

His eyebrows went up. "Eh? Bibles? She is the religious enthusiast? The martyr for the faith?"

I nodded.

He shook his head. "A pity. Actually, your American Christians would accomplish much more if they were not so selfish, like the rest of...excuse me, mon ami. I meant, if they were not always waiting for miracles. But no matter. I take it you are to be the mademoiselle's miracle?"

I chuckled. "I don't know what she's praying for, but I'm what she's getting. Now, my venerated friend who loves the sad gaiety of Paris, what have you heard?"

He thought a moment. "Arrangements?"

I grinned. This was always part of our little dance. "The usual amount in the usual account." All I knew was that a certain amount of cash...something scandalous, no doubt...was transferred electronically to a numbered account in Zurich whenever we received useful information from LeChance.

He nodded, satisfied. The he shrugged. "About the mademoiselle, I know only what you have just told me. About Romania...does the name Lubenkoff mean anything to you?"

I shook my head. "The last time I was there, the contact was Wormbrud. Now it's a Russian?"

"Oui. He lives in Bucharest, next door to the American embassy and, er...receives gifts, if you take my meaning, from every government who can reach him. They all know about it, but most of them believe he feeds the others misinformation."

"And in truth?"

"In truth, mon ami, he always tells everyone the absolute truth. This is poetic, is it not?"

# *Chapter 4*

O n the plane I thought about how to contact Lubenkoff without being seen around the American embassy. Any activity over there would raise suspicions.

The Bucharest airport was good preparation for the city itself: dismal. Inadequate lighting hid the film that covered almost everything. Stocky, middle-aged women in washed-out babushkas pushed ancient brooms without bristles. They wrapped dirty, wet towels around the things and stayed busy.

Outside, I still hadn't come up with a good alternative, so I just found my way to Lubenkoff's neighborhood without trying to be devious or clever about it. His home was really my only option, since I knew nothing of his habits.

After all, I didn't know what he looked like! My only choice was to meet him at home...without being seen.

I wandered around the vicinity of the embassy, going from shop to pub to restaurant, slowly changing clothes in men's rooms and fitting rooms. This went on until I'd dumped my business suit and wore my "basic black" outfit: turtleneck sweater, black jeans, black Navy boondocker shoes.

When the sun went down, I walked around the same block four times, making sure no one was watching. Then I crossed the street, to the embassy's block, and slipped over the chain link fence. I was now at the end of a long row of what passed for back yards. Fortunately, pets weren't common in these countries. That meant the only real obstacles between the yard and me were rickety fences, discarded furniture and rats.

I wasn't worried about anyone looking out a back window. There was nothing to see. For most, the evening ritual had begun: a meager meal of turnip soup, black bread and cheese, followed by as much bootlegged vodka as possible. Oblivion brought temporary relief.

I moved slowly, giving the rats time to get away from me without panicking. Too much squealing and scrambling could encourage someone to put his glass down and look out a window.

Red eyes glared at me as the little furry bodies scurried away in the dark. I had to move carefully around the debris, not wanting to surprise anything.

By the time I got to the yard I wanted, I was biting back the impulse to shoot them. One or two rats wouldn't bother me, but these multitudes made my skin crawl. Where did they go during the day?

By counting fences, I made it to the right yard and found that the cellar door was suitably rotten and splintery, and its lock was agreeably breakable.

Once in the cellar, it was time for the penlight. There was no way my eyes would adjust to the comparative total blackness down there.

As my eyes adjusted to the sudden stab of light, the floor seemed to undulate in a surge of movement in every direction at once. Now I knew where the rats went. They seemed to be about six deep, all scrambling in different directions.

It took forty-five minutes to cross the room to the stairway that led to the first landing. I should have done it in thirty seconds, but the whole city would have known I was there. I took another fifteen minutes trying to keep the stairs from creaking as I climbed.

The door at the top wasn't locked at all. Most folks were too smart to try going down here.

Now it was time for the interesting part. Which of the eight apartments in this building was Lubenkoff's?

Top floor...he could hear people coming. He had the roof if he needed it.

That narrowed the apartments down to two. From there, I just had to remember which side of this building was closer to the embassy.

The stairs up here were in better shape, and carpeted. I made it all the way to the top in record time. Approaching the top floor was the slowest.

Guys like this one, playing both ends against the middle, had to have an alarm system.

This one was pretty predictable. Every third step was wired. I still wasn't sure whether surprise would help me. I'd been trying to keep others from knowing I was here. What about him? Would it be better to announce my presence and let him think he had the advantage?

No, I decided. Keep as many people as far off balance as possible. That was my style, and it worked.

His apartment was locked. I wanted him off-balance, but not hostile. So much for breaking down the flimsy wooden door.

I stood outside his apartment and listened for a bit. He was shuffling around. I wanted to rush in, but I held back. Too soon, too soon. If he already has company, I'll ruin everything. Make sure he's alone. Give him time to talk to someone.

Reassured that he was alone, I gave the door four hard raps.

"Eh?" I heard. Then footsteps, followed by something guttural that I didn't understand.

"Lubenkoff!" I whispered, just loud enough for his ears. "Open up! Hurry!"

"'Hurry! Hurry!' you say. Yes, I can see that you are an American. Why do I need to see you in such a hurry?"

"I won't leave you alone until you do! Right now I'm in a race against the clock. Soon you will have to join me!" It was a gamble that he had an appointment my presence would spoil. The door was immediately unlocked and opened.

Lubenkoff was no longer young, and that was really his only distinguishing feature. Medium height, a plain face, vague gestures. This guy could get lost in a crowd of two. That would be an advantage, considering his profession.

"So, Mr. Ugly," he said, closing the door, "now we race against the clock together. What is it you wish?"

There was no point in beating around any bushes. "The Cuban physicist's daughter. I need to know where she's being held."

A look of fear swept across his face, followed by a craftiness that stayed there. "Ah! This is something that everybody races against the clock for, no? My government wants the physicist, so does yours, he wants his daughter, she wants her freedom, and everyone is in a hurry. Well! You are asking for something dangerous, Mr. Ugly American. Your Uncle will have to be rich indeed!"

"Well, let me show you. I know all about hidden weapons and devices for protection, so I want you to know I'm going for my billfold."

He nodded. "Please do so."

I pulled it out of my hip pocket and handed it to him, slowly. "It's all yours for the information."

He opened it and noticed the Russian currency. "You give me rubles?" he said, surprised.

"I realize dollars are worth more, but you would have a harder time explaining them."

He nodded again. "All mine, eh?"

"For the information," I pointed out.

The gun came out from under his jacket as he made his wild bid for easy money. Before he could aim, my left hand grabbed his gun hand and my right hand had the same forearm, squeezing hard. Fingers in pain, he couldn't squeeze the trigger.

"All I have to do," I said, "is pretend I'm squeezing out a wet cloth, and your right hand will be useless for the rest of your life! We know how much the information is worth to me; now how much is it worth to you?" I began to twist his wrist. He winced.

He looked much older now. Wrinkles and pockmarks appeared as sweat broke out on his face. He began to babble an address. I stopped him with another squeeze. "That means nothing to me. Directions!"

The pain was in his eyes. His imagination was neutralized. He couldn't think up any lies. The directions came quickly, and I let him go. His numbed fingers nearly dropped the gun. I plucked it easily out of his hand. A little Beretta. Oh, well. Better than nothing.

"I don't think I'll stay for dinner," I said, stepping to his door. "I'll give you time to hide the rubles from your next guest. Goodbye, Lubenkoff."

As I left the building by the front entrance, I repeated his directions to myself while I strapped his little gun to my calf. I'd come prepared.

# *Chapter 5*

Lubenkoff's directions were surprisingly good. It only took me a few minutes of walking to find the building Carmen Gonsalo was being held in.

They were taking special care of her. She was being held in one of those nameless, faceless high-rise apartment buildings that littered all of Eastern Europe. It was simply a matter of walking into the lobby like I owned the place and marching to the elevator. I stepped into it and pressed the button for the top floor: the eighteenth. Several people entered behind me. Some of them were security goons, but I was ready for them.

People got on and off as we slowly ascended through the building. By the seventeenth floor, I was almost alone. Two men stayed on the inside of the doors to make sure no one got off. That was a bit obvious since I was the only other one there. At the top floor, I got off and one of them joined me. As the doors closed, he stepped in front of me and said, in accented English, "You do not live on this floor!"

"Neither do you!" I said.

The unaccustomed insolence was too much for him. As he reached for me, I caught him. I grabbed his chin in one hand and the back of his head with the other. He had a split second of realization before I twisted and wrenched his head as hard and fast as I could.

He slumped to the floor. I fished through his pockets as the death rattle shook him slightly. I felt a moment of regret. After all, this wasn't Maria Maltevar or some traitor. But I couldn't afford to have him regain consciousness before I had the job done...more than one life would be neutralized in that case, so I chose to hate myself for a while.

I found a holster cradling a .357 Magnum. A bit of a relic, and definitely not standard issue here, but better than Lubenkoff's peashooter. Considering the addition a return of stolen goods, I left the little Beretta under the strap around my calf. Then I stuffed the Magnum under my belt at the small of my back, under my sweater.

Don't linger, Donley. Time is an enemy. I glanced around and found a kind of lounge area for residents. It used to be an apartment. I dragged him into one of the chairs in a far corner of the room. Then it was time to move on.

The stairs to the roof were easy to find. However, I'd forgotten about the housemaids that were stationed on every floor. Fortunately, they were sitting in their room with the door open, smoking and watching television and being generally oblivious. By moving past their room at just the right speed, I remained invisible to them.

The entrance to the roof was locked, but no challenge, and I soon stepped into the night air. I took a moment to look down at the lights of the city. Not nearly what you'd see in New York or even Paris, but it was a city.

I found Carmen's corner and leaned over. Every suite in these buildings has a little balcony. Hers had no one stationed on it. They were confident we wouldn't pull something so suicidal. I hoisted myself over and swung so my feet were heading inward, over the railing and onto her balcony.

For a bad moment, I was sure I'd miscalculated and there would be a Donley-splat on the pavement. But my body behaved itself and went right over the rail.

My landing sounded thunderous to me, but no one inside seemed to notice. I crept up to the glass doors and peered through the sheer curtain.

# *Chapter 6*

A young woman with olive skin and long, black hair was on her knees next to a cot against one wall, with her hands in the air. All things considered, I felt safe in assuming it was Carmen Gonsalo.

She was crying, but under control. She didn't look like she'd been mistreated. However, her face showed that she'd been having a rough time.

"Father," I heard her say through the glass, "I don't pretend to understand why this happened, but I'm trusting You to work it out for Your glory." Her voice came in between gasping sobs that she tried to suppress. "Please forgive me for being angry about it at first and help me to have a better attitude; to be a better witness for You. In the mighty Name of Jesus, Amen."

"Father". Yeah, I remember that. When my mother had prayed, her favorite word had been "Father". It seemed to fill her with warm fuzzies.

Not me. "Father" was a vague shape with a loud voice, always angry. Then one day he just wasn't there anymore. I never learned where he went or why, and didn't care. I did remember my mother crying a lot. She never talked about him again except in the most formal terms. There never was any "daddy", "dad", or "pop"...just "your father". By the time I was old enough to say "my father", the term was irrelevant.

I shook my head and focused. This was no time for self-therapy.

The door to the hall opened and a heavy-set woman entered. She had a pale complexion and wore the ever-present brown uniform. Obviously, this was Carmen's keeper. She carried a tray that held a bowl, a slice of bread and a cup.

Carmen jumped up and said, "Jesus loves you anyway, Nadia."

Nadia ignored her. "Here's something to eat. Be quick. They are waiting for the dishes downstairs."

The captive approached the table happily, saying, "Oh, thank You, Jesus!"

That roused Nadia. "I will have you know," she pronounced, "that it was the communist party that provided this food for you, not this Jesus of yours. If you want to thank someone, thank the communist party." Then she stood with a mixture of pride and disapproval, having made her point.

"Oh, I see," Carmen said. It was hard to tell what her attitude was. She looked Nadia straight in the eye and said, "Can I leave now?"

Nadia got even huffier. "Of course not! Do not be ridiculous!"

Carmen gave her a contemptuous look and said, "Well, thank you, communist party!" Then she sat down and started eating.

Shrugging, Nadia turned and started to leave. I nearly tapped at the window. Suddenly she turned and glared at Carmen. "I cannot understand why you persist in this foolish belief," she said, "Do you not know that this is the twentieth century!"

The captive looked up. "The twentieth century since what?"

"Why...since...since..." When she realized it, she rolled her eyes and looked disgusted. "Since Jesus!" she spat out.

Now Carmen was standing again, pointing her finger and using words like daggers. "Exactly! Every time you write the date you acknowledge Jesus Christ, whether you like it or not!"

"Meaningless words!" Nadia parried. "It will take more than that turn me into such a fool as to...to allow myself to be oppressed by the ruling classes by...by believing that some God will reward me when I'm dead!"

Carmen countered with, "Well, if I'm so oppressed, and you're so enlightened, what are you all afraid of me for? Why am I the one who's being kept behind locked doors? And as for which one of us is the fool, the answer to that was written centuries ago!"

Nadia was stepping into a hole, but her curiosity was too strong. "What's that?"

"Psalm fourteen, verse one: 'The fool hath said in his heart, there is no God!'"

That did it for Nadia. She turned to the door, said something like, "Ugh!" and was gone.

I waited, to be sure she wasn't outside the door thinking of another futile comeback. Meanwhile, Carmen left my field of vision and returned with a potted plant. While she admired it, I tapped on the window. She heard, looked, gasped, and came over. No fear, apprehension or caution. Well, what did she have to lose?

When the sliding door was open, I stepped inside and looked around, ready to leave immediately.

"Who...who are you?" she asked, her eyes wide.

I loved those moments. Shine up the white armor, polish up the halo, and charge to the rescue...but I knew better. Besides, there wasn't time.

"The cavalry," I answered, "coming over the hill. Pack your things, Carmen. Let's go home."

Her eyes got wider. "You're...you're an American!"

"Very good. You got it right the first time. Now can we please..."

"But...how did you get in here?"

I bit back what I was going to say and came back with, "I just stepped in from the balcony; where were you?"

"I mean...this is the seventeenth floor!"

"Right. Nice and close to the roof. A little Tarzan action and voila! Here I am."

That actually calmed her down. "Oh." Then she remembered something. "But...but there are guards!"

Okay, Donley. Now's your chance to show the damsel in distress what an awesome super spy you are. I snickered. "Well, there's one less guard now."

I never found out what she thought of that. She cocked her head to one side and said, "Shh! Someone's coming!"

"Oh, great!" I muttered, in disgust. Between the element of surprise and the accumulated firepower, I could probably have blasted my way out of the building, with Carmen in tow. But public violence would give them an excuse to call out the heavy artillery to stop the American killer. As long as I kept it to a simple rescue operation, they'd be unwilling to acknowledge that it ever even happened. I'd have to play it coy.

A quick look around showed me that the balcony was the only place to go. Stepping back through, I said, "You won't forget I'm out here, will you?"

She shook her head and closed the door as the hallway door opened. There was just enough time for her to step away and glare at Nadia, who was leading a young, intimidated girl into the room.

# Chapter 7

"Miss Gonsalo," Nadia said, "this is Olga. She will be available to help you if you need anything while I am busy."

Carmen struck a pose. "Well, if you really want to know what I need..."

"Within reason, of course. Olga, clean up her things. I will be down the hall if you need me." Her tone indicated that she didn't expect or desire to be needed any time soon.

A high pitched, frightened little voice said, "Y...yes, comrade."

Nadia did an about-face and left, shutting the door behind her. Carmen was left alone with Olga.

This had all the signs of a trap. I just couldn't figure out why. They knew where she stood; what could they want from her?

After a few awkward seconds Olga said, "I...I am told you...believe in...in Jesus."

Carmen jumped for that bait. "Why, yes. Not only do I believe in Him; I have a personal relationship with Him."

Olga was changing. I wasn't sure I liked that. She seemed as eager to talk about this as Carmen was. "Yes, I know. Once I knew someone who...well, he spoke like that."

Carmen was interested. "What happened?"

"I...I don't know. One day he just wasn't there anymore."

Carmen shook her head. "I'm amazed at you people over here. Can't you see?"

Olga looked confused. She didn't see. "See what?"

"See the obvious!" Carmen said, "No one ever tries to break into East Berlin. No boat people tried to get into Vietnam or Cambodia. No one goes to Russia and asks for political asylum. You're telling me about someone you knew who just disappeared because of what he believed."

"I did not say it was because of what he believed!"

"Oh, come now!"

Olga studied the floor for a moment before saying, "Does...does everyone in America believe in Jesus?"

Carmen shook her head, her eyes getting wide. "Oh, no! We get laughed at quite a bit. A lot of Christians don't share their faith because of that."

Olga became indignant. "If getting laughed at was the only risk, I would share my faith with everyone!"

Carmen's voice got soft, but her words went for the jugular. "What is your faith, Olga? Do you believe in the communist party?"

That flustered her. "N...no, I...I..." Then she must have realized who she was talking to. "It feeds me! It..."

"Wait a minute. It might feed you, but it imprisoned me." Carmen countered, "And you are avoiding my question. Why did you say 'no' at first?"

Olga stammered. "Well, this neighbor...he was so peaceful; so confident. He always said, 'I know whom I have believed, and am persuaded that He is able to...to...'"

Carmen picked it up. "...to keep that which I've committed unto Him against that day."

"How did you know that?"

"It's from God's Word, the Bible. And it's really true, Olga. God does take care of us."

"He...He does not seem to do a very good job," Olga observed, echoing my own thoughts.

"Oh, doesn't He?" Carmen countered. "What's the worst thing that can happen to me?"

"You can be killed!"

I couldn't help but think, "Yeah!"

Carmen turned and stepped away from her. "And I'll be with Christ forever. That's nothing to be afraid of."

Olga said, "You...you could be tortured, or...or maimed! You could...lose a limb..."

Carmen turned back and looked at her. "Olga, you can make the road rocky, but it still ends at heaven."

*Oh, brother!* I thought. But it reached Olga.

She said, "I...I would love to have such confidence."

Carmen was ready. "All you need is Jesus in your heart. He will give you everything you need."

Olga's face showed a mixture of eagerness and fear. "How...how..."

"You only need to ask Him," Carmen urged her. "Would you like me to help you?"

I shivered...it was getting chilly out here...as Olga nodded silently.

They prayed, Carmen leading and Olga repeating. It went something like this:

"Lord Jesus, I'm sorry for my sins. Please come into my heart and make me a new person. I believe You died for me, and rose again from the dead, and will guide me until I come home to be with You. Amen."

Carmen grinned from ear to ear. "I'd give you a Romanian Bible, but they were all confiscated."

Olga grinned back. She even looked different. "Do not worry. Now that I know where I stand, I will get one!"

I heard a distant voice but couldn't understand what it said.

Olga scrambled to pick up the dishes with the half-eaten food and called out, "Coming!"

I heard Carmen say, "Oh, thank You, Jesus!" as I tapped on the glass. She said "Oh!" and came running.

The guard's Magnum was in my hand as I stepped into the room after she opened the door. I couldn't help shivering a little. "You picked a fine time to preach a sermon!" I said.

She was smiling, radiant. "It was worth it."

"That's easy for you to say," I countered, waving my arms. "I was the one out there in the wind!"

She noticed the gun at that point, and said, "What's that?"

I played innocent. "What's what?"

She pointed and spat out, "That!"

Well, I have to admit it was a sloppy evasion, but I couldn't respect the way she pretended she didn't know what a gun was. "Oh, this?" I said, holding it up. "It's an eraser. Remember those guards we talked about? It used to belong to one of them. Come on now, let's go."

"Not while you've got that thing."

Great. Just what I needed: a rabid pacifist.

"Look," I said, "We really don't have time to argue about it right now. Let's just..."

"No!" She was getting upset. "These people might get saved some day, and I won't let you take their lives on my account."

"I'm not trying to take their lives. I'm trying to save yours!"

"No! Get rid of that thing!"

I'd played this out as far as I could. The flowerpot she'd put on the table earlier gave me an idea. I could appease her pacifistic tendencies and leave a trap at the same time. "Okay," I said, "if it'll get us out of here any faster..." I stuck the barrel into the soil in the flowerpot, twisted it twice, and pulled it out. Then I showed her the clogged barrel and laid the gun on the table. "There. If I tried to shoot now, it would backfire and blow my face off. I couldn't use it if I wanted to. Now, can we please leave this place?"

Finally she was ready. I got behind her and gently herded her in the right direction, hoping she wouldn't find something else to make an issue of.

We had just reached the window when I heard movement behind us. A familiar voice said, "Stop...or I shoot!"

# Chapter 8

I turned and saw Nadia glaring at me, holding the Magnum in both hands. The soil-packed barrel seemed to be smiling at me. I couldn't help chuckling as I stepped away from Carmen, saying, "I wouldn't shoot that thing if I were you."

Carmen, who could also see the barrel, was upset. "Please! Don't shoot!" she almost screamed.

Out of the corner of my eye I saw Olga step in, size up the situation, and reach for the light switch. A moment later the room was in darkness. I could feel the tension from Nadia, and I knew how she was reacting, so I put a hand over my eyes and squeezed them shut.

The explosion rocked the room. Carmen screamed. I opened my eyes just before Olga turned the light back on.

Nadia's body was sprawled on the floor. What had been her head was a mess of red and grey pulp. Her right arm was thrown out, the remains of the hand glistening wetly.

The others hadn't closed their eyes. The flash had blinded them. Their eyes still hadn't adjusted.

Olga said, "Oh, I...I did not think she would shoot with the light off!" I could have told her better, but I kept my mouth shut.

Then she saw the body. There was no shock or disgust, just surprise. She looked at Carmen and said, "He does take care of us!"

Carmen's eyes were adjusting, too. When she noticed the corpse, her face went through several changes. First the shock and disgust I didn't see on Olga's, then she looked like she was going to cry. She shuddered, and a few tears spilled down her face. Olga was nervous and impatient. Carmen didn't notice. She knelt down by Nadia's feet, and her face looked stricken with a hopeless longing. "Oh, Nadia..." She stayed there for a few moments, silently weeping.

I was getting crazier than ever to just get out, but I knew this would be the wrong moment to push, so I kept my mouth shut.

Finally, she turned away and glared at me. The sorrow was replaced by a smoldering fury. "You did that!"

I rolled my eyes and held my hands up in a sign of helplessness. "Hey, I didn't make her shoot!"

She wasn't about to get off her track. She took another step toward me and said, "How can she get saved now?"

It looked like some kind of hysterical fit was coming. I wasn't sure what to do about it. I could knock her out and carry her, but that would get very awkward very soon.

Olga rescued me. "Please go now; do not wait any longer!" she said. "I must report your escape, but I will wait as long as I can. Please hurry!"

"The girl makes sense," I said. "Let's go!"

Without another word, we went to the door. Olga stepped aside silently and let us pass. The stairs were just a few feet to the left. Just before stepping into the hall, I checked the little Beretta, still safe in the calf strap.

# Chapter 9

I wasn't nearly as subtle leaving as I'd been coming, but now speed was the main thing.

In the lobby, everyone was talking. We heard the English words, "dead body" several times. She looked at me, and her face told me the rest of this job wasn't going to be easy.

I grabbed her elbow and said, "Come on! We can't afford to stand around here waiting for someone to recognize you!"

She pulled her elbow away roughly. "Don't touch me!"

"Then don't make it necessary! Let's go!"

I turned and hurried toward the entrance, trying to maintain a casual air. If she didn't follow on her own, I'd have to somehow knock her out and carry her after all. She could hate my guts all she wanted to...once I got her to safety.

It wasn't necessary. Her footsteps were right there, behind me. She didn't want to catch up, but she was back there.

We threaded our way through narrow side streets until I found a run-down clothing store. I knocked on the door loudly, yelling, "Open up!"

She caught up with me, panicked. "What are you doing?"

"We need new clothes. We look too American."

"But...but they'll remember us! They'll...they'll..."

"They'll help us. These people hate their Russian masters a lot more than we understand."

A light went on, a male voice bellowed something I didn't understand, and a grizzled face appeared at the door. I saw his mouth make the word "American?" I nodded vigorously. Quickly, he opened the door and ushered us inside.

"I help Amerikains," he announced. "What you need?"

"We need clothes," I said. "We will trade what we are wearing," I indicated our clothes, trying to use as much body language as possible, "for your clothes...from your racks."

Carmen was scandalized again...or still. I wasn't sure which. "Used clothes for new? You're cheating him!"

"Don't be stupid!" I countered. "He'll make more selling this stuff than he would in a year with what he has."

The store was dark, a study of black and grey and shifting shadows. He moved around the room quickly, confidently selecting things he could barely see. I knew it would be bargain-basement quality at home, but it was top-of-the-line here.

Carmen was ushered into the fitting room first. He continued searching for my "new" clothes, humming tunelessly until she stepped out.

It was quite a transformation. A brown, shapeless dress under a grey coat with an equally shapeless hat covering her hair. She grinned ruefully--she was forgetting she didn't like me--and said, "Well, hallelujah anyhow."

Her face was wrong for the outfit, but there was nothing I could do about that. It wasn't just that she was pretty. It was the joy in her face, and her vulnerability mixed with strength. The whole effect touched a part of me that I'd kept buried as long as I could remember. I felt like I wanted to give her permission to hurt me, but protect her fiercely from all would-be attackers. I did not enjoy these feelings.

Our host's eyes lit up. "Hallelujah?" he questioned, from her to me and back again. "Hallelujah?"

Carmen got excited. "Yes, thank You, Jesus!"

Well, that sure put a quick end to my need for a cold shower. I couldn't help thinking, here we go again!

He then said something that sounded like "Yay-zu!"

I decided that three was a crowd, so I grabbed my pile of clothes and went to the fitting room while they had their happy time. While I changed, my discomfort melted and I saw that we probably had an ally now. I wasn't sure exactly what that meant just yet, but it was encouraging.

When I returned, she was telling him about Olga, trying to get him to get in touch with her somehow.

"Very clever!" I bit out. "Why don't you just leave a trail of breadcrumbs for them to follow?"

She made a face at me and said, "This is more important. Besides, it's what I'm here for."

"Fine," I said. "Getting you out alive is what I'm here for, and you're not helping."

The old man was struggling to follow our dialogue, but he'd caught something. "Get...out? Get out? Where you go?"

Carmen looked at me. I shrugged and said, "Out of the country, and that's more than he needs to know." I was planning to take her to Greece, through Bulgaria, but nobody else had to know that.

He frowned at that, thought for a moment, and finally held a hand up, heading for the back room.

I said, "I hope you realize you're putting both him and us in danger by letting him know so much." Not that I was broken up about it, of course, but I did try to keep collateral damage down when I could. Besides, I thought that by showing some concern for someone's life, I might make her more cooperative.

She didn't look at me. Making a pretense of examining the merchandise, she said, "If you don't need my approval for what you do, then I don't need your approval for what I do."

Before I could throw anything back at her, he returned. In one hand, he held a map. In the other was something small and shiny.

A car key.

He held the map so we could all see it and pointed to a red dot off the road about three miles south of the city, and then pressed the map into my hands. He ushered us to the door, saying, "Go...wit...Gott."

Carmen beamed at him. "Thank you, my brother...for everything."

"Brother", she'd called him. That was something else I didn't know about. To start with, I was an only child. Siblings were never anything I wanted, either. I'd never seen any siblings who really got along.

People tell me that attitudes like that change when you're an adult. Not for me. I still didn't want any siblings. My mind hadn't changed.

And anybody who thought my profession was a brotherhood of any kind ought to get kicked in the head. Nobody ever braved enemy fire for a fallen comrade. In fact, we had a hard time getting along at all when we had to work in teams. Fortunately, it didn't happen often.

This brash kid spends an hour with someone she can't even really talk to and he's her "brother".

I hadn't felt so awkward, clumsy and...well...wrong...in years.

I jammed the shapeless hat on to my head and stepped outside. We had a lot of walking to do.

The street left the city and became a gravel road, with small, look-alike houses on either side. The 'burbs, Romanian style. Here's where government officials with families lived. The singles, much like their western counterparts, preferred the city with its social opportunities.

Carmen seemed to bury the hatchet. "I used to dream about living in the country. I'd go crazy, living so far away from people and their needs. And after seeing this...I mean, how people live in countries like this, Brooklyn seems like Paradise."

I snorted. "Hell itself might look like Paradise next to this place."

The wistful smile vanished, and she stiffened up again. I had a real talent for saying the wrong things to this girl.

# Chapter 10

The red dot turned out to be a grove of trees twenty feet off the main road with a pile of broken branches covering up an old Volvo. We uncovered it and I got into the driver's seat. After a few tries, the engine finally turned over and we were ready to roll.

Carmen slipped into the passenger seat and we were off. She still had a triumphant attitude, in spite of her weariness. "Now we just drive to safety?" she asked. The tone of her voice told me she knew that was wrong; this was her way of asking what to expect next.

I shook my head. "First we have a border to cross."

"A border to cross? How do we do that?"

I shrugged. "I don't know yet."

And I really didn't know. There are many ways, of course. We could trot into the woods and cut through, but we didn't have time for that. All the fastest ways involved leaving dead border guards behind. If she saw any more of that from me, she'd probably go running back to her "friends" in Romania. I wanted to make sure she stayed with me. I'd have to either figure out something brilliant...or knock her out.

About two hours later, the little guardhouses and roadblocks came into view. I still hadn't thought of anything, brilliant or otherwise, when she said, "I still don't know your name."

I bit back all the tempting sarcastic remarks and told her simply, "Bill. Bill Donley."

"Bill, do you...do you mind if I handle the guards?"

"You?!"

She looked defiant. "Well, I managed to get into these countries without any trouble, and with a suitcase full of Bibles. They didn't catch me until a week later, when I was giving away the last ones."

"I thought you said they were confiscated."

"They were. The man who told me he wanted one was really in the KGB, or whatever they call their secret police here. Anyway, let me try."

I waged an internal war until conceding that I didn't have anything better...except dead border guards.

I sighed and said, "Okay. We'll give it a shot."

That made her so happy she forgot who I was, or that I was even there. She smiled at some private thought, closed her eyes and put her head down. She stayed that way all the way through what followed.

Since traffic was almost at a standstill, I found myself watching her as she sat there in her privacy. That protective, almost possessive sense welled up in me again. I could not, would not reach over and stroke her hair like I suddenly wanted to so badly. With the realization, my throat filled up and I was groaning in pain...and confused by the whole sensation. I shook my head violently.

Her eyes opened, alarmed. "What? What happened?"

"Nothing happened," I said, too forcefully. "Everything's just fine."

Her look said she didn't believe me. Then she closed her eyes and put her head down again.

I focused on the scenario outside the car from then on. That was a lot safer...for me, anyway.

There were two cars ahead of us. The guards, brandishing their AK-47s, ordered everyone out of the first car.

A family of five climbed out and stood off to the side of the road, angry but intimidated.

Then the luggage came out and was placed on the ground. One of the guards opened the suitcases and pulled everything out, one piece at a time, and threw it over his shoulder. The other guard got into the car and I couldn't see what he did.

The suitcase guard finished his destruction and ordered the family to replace everything. The children ran to the stuff first, then the mother. When the father moved to join them, the guard tripped him and laughed as he went sprawling. That was the price of not having anything worth confiscating.

I began to hope fervently that they would try something like that on me.

Then the guard in the car was finished and they were ordered to move on. They were still re-packing. The guards yelled at them until they just shoved everything into something and got back into their car.

The car in front of us pulled up and two men got out. The suitcase routine started again. This time the other guard took out a screwdriver and began to remove the inside of the driver's door.

They really seemed to enjoy their work, those two.

I heard an exclamation from over by the suitcases and saw the guard holding two bottles of booze. The passenger indicated that he should keep one, which he did. The other bottle went back into the suitcase. It was then closed. The guard called to the other one, who muttered and fumed, but replaced all the screws. When the car drove off, the screwdriver guard yelled at the suitcase guard, who yelled back.

As this escalated to a major shouting match, I muttered, "Now what?"

Carmen stirred and said, "Just drive. Slowly."

Well, it was her day in the sun. I put the car in gear and rolled slowly past the two of them. They were so busy turning purple with rage they didn't even look at us.

After I drove for five more minutes, Carmen snapped out of it. "See?" she challenged. "That works a whole lot better than just killing everyone in sight!"

Again, the unfairness of the accusation hit me. If I'd killed everyone in sight, things probably would have gone a lot easier from the start.

There was a question in my mind, and I spoke that out instead. "What works better?"

She smiled sweetly. "Prayer," she said.

# *Chapter 11*

The rest of the drive was outwardly uneventful. Inside, I was fighting. "Prayer." She'd been gambling everything on the God of my mother.

But with all of Mom's slavish devotion to this God, He'd never seemed to come through for her. At least, not like what I had just seen. I would always wonder why He'd seemed so silent when I was young. After this episode I'd never be able to simply dismiss His existence again.

The shack I wanted was still there. It stood in the middle of the clearing like a forgotten scar. This was the rendezvous point. The last time I'd been here was right after setting fire to a building containing biological warfare experiments. I never heard about any weird illnesses around here, so I guess I'd torched it in time.

I wasn't really happy with this place. We'd used it once too often for my taste. It was supposed to be a safe house, but I didn't feel safe, so I took my usual precautions.

I left Carmen outside, slipped the Beretta into my hand where she couldn't see it and took a slow breath. Then I turned the doorknob, pushed the door open and rolled in. I hit the far wall and turned, ready to shoot.

The empty, silent room seemed to smirk back at me. It had a table and two chairs in the middle of the room. An old military cot was against one wall, a worn easy chair against another. Nothing else. I called out, "It's okay, Carmen. Come on in." I was preoccupied, but I slipped the Beretta into my pocket before she could see it.

She entered, looked around and sank into one of the chairs at the table. "Well, now what?"

I made sure the blackout curtain was down and lit a candle. "Now we wait for a helicopter that'll take us over the border into Greece. Then you'll go home to papa and I'll go on vacation. Happy ending all around."

She gave me a funny look. "Vacation? What does a...someone like you...do on a vacation?"

This was getting a little too personal and friendly for me, so I growled, "That's confidential information."

She said something like, "Hmmphh," and looked unimpressed.

"I can't think about that right now anyway," I went on, to keep her from getting back on personal things. "First I have to make sure we don't have to pay the smuggler's ransom."

She looked puzzled. "'Smuggler's ransom'?"

"Yeah. You're the smuggler. Your father's the ransom. Your little crusade of religious idealism has hurt a lot of people, particularly your own father. When those Romanian dirtbags you love so much and hate to see killed, found out who you are, they sent a blackmail note to Washington. They wanted us to hand over your dad to them, after which they promised to let you go. History has taught the world not to trust the promises those people make, so I was sent instead. Think about it." I was annoyed at her attitude of moral superiority. After all, I wasn't the one who'd caused all this trouble; she was.

"'Smuggler's ransom', huh?" she repeated.

Steamed, I let it go without an answer.

A sly smile spread across her face and she said, slowly, "Actually, I've already been ransomed."

"Wha...?" It took a second to dawn on me, and then I realized what she was doing. "Uh-oh, I got a feeling I know what's coming."

"Oh, be serious for a minute. Let me show you." She pulled a little Bible...in English...out of a pocket and flipped through it. "In Matthew, chapter 20, verse 28, Jesus says, 'just as the Son of Man did not come to be served, but to serve, and to give His life a ransom for many.'"

I wasn't about to make this easy for her, so I countered with, "'A ransom for many'? How do you know that includes you?"

She didn't take offense. In fact, she became even more animated. "First of all, because I've received Him as my Master and He never turns anyone away who comes honestly." She flipped through the Book and found another spot. "Also, the Apostle Paul expanded the idea when he wrote to Timothy. Here: 'For there is one God and one Mediator between God and men, the Man Christ Jesus, who gave Himself a ransom for all...'" She'd slowed down on the last four words, then she went on, "'...to be testified in due time.' That's in First Timothy, chapter 2, and verses 5 and 6. You see, I know I'm going to heaven when I die. I've been ransomed by the death of Christ. It's for everybody, but you have to take it."

She was making me uncomfortable, but I wasn't about to drop it yet. I wanted to needle her some more. "You're trying to tell me I'm going to hell, is that it?"

She smiled, like a teacher with a struggling pupil. "I can't judge you," she said, "I'm trying to tell you that I know I'm going to heaven. You can know it also, by accepting the price that's been paid for you."

Absently I said, "Yeah, I heard what you said to what's-her-name."

"Olga," she volunteered.

"Yeah." This wasn't going right. I needed to change the direction somehow. Then I got an idea. Leaning on the table, I said, "What I don't understand is this thing you have about guns. What does that have to do with anything?"

I could see that I'd caught her off guard. She stammered, "I...I'm sure you'll think this is really a corny way to look at life, but I don't know how else to say it. Millions of people die without Christ every day, and I can only reach a very small number of them. If any of these people get killed, they'll never have a chance to get saved. I can't let that happen."

I almost mentioned that it had already happened on this operation without her permission, but decided against it. Instead, I said, "Listen. When I was in the military, I had to go to chapel every Sunday in boot camp. There was one chaplain who talked just like you." I had no intention of actually saying the next sentence. It just burst out without my permission. "I hated his guts." Well, there it was. I decided to push on. "Anyway, he never once told us we'd have to resign from the service; he was in it himself! What about that?"

"Well...at least soldiers don't kill in cold blood like you do!"

"Okay, let's make it personal then. Suppose some terrorist was getting ready to throw acid in a child's face, and the only way you could stop him was to kill him. What would you do?"

It worked. She lost it. "I don't know!" She stood up and threw her arms into the air. "I'd like to say I'd pray and get a miracle, but I honestly don't know!"

Well, now that I'd won I could afford to be generous. "Okay, forget it, kid. No hard feelings. Try to get some sleep before the chopper gets here."

She gave me a reproachful look, sat back down, made a cradle of her arms and put her head down without a word.

There was a bench in the corner. I made myself as comfortable as possible. I don't know how much time went by before I finally drifted off.

# *Chapter 12*

My mother was there again. She was leaning forward in a chair with that big, loving smile. "Billy! Billy!" she called.

I stopped playing to look up at her and smiled back. "Yes, Mommy?"

The memory usually broke off there, but this time it continued. Her face lit up even more and she said, "Billy, Jesus loves you!"

Suddenly I was awake, sweating and shaking. I didn't know why; it wasn't a shocking revelation. I knew what my background was.

I'd successfully submerged all those memories for years. For a while it was all I could think of, and a raging fury would well up within me at the God who'd taken my mother away. Then I'd switched tactics and ignored Him, filling up my mind and emotions by choosing a lifestyle with a kill-or-be-killed urgency.

Now suddenly I was wide awake in a silent room in a quiet moment, with nowhere to hide.

I got up and paced quietly, trying not to wake Carmen up.

Poor mom. She was always saying things like that. She tried so hard to get me to believe. I did, too...until she died, anyway. I was twelve, just hitting puberty and life was hard enough, and then she was gone. The world then became too hard, too cruel for me to believe in and follow a loving God anymore.

I thought I had to be harder and meaner than the world around me to survive. I rejected the most lasting and valuable thing she gave me: her faith.

Carmen stirred, mumbled something in her sleep, and relaxed again. Looking at her, I felt like an observer, watching my growing and unwelcome attraction for her give way to a more important and urgent issue.

Amazing. She knows she's a pawn in an international chess game, and yet she sleeps like a baby. I haven't slept that well in years.

And when she talks about God! Part of me wants to believe her and part of me wants to smack her. I thought I was immune to propaganda. Why does this Jesus business bother me like that?

I knew the answer, of course. I just wanted to pretend I didn't. The pull was there, like a magnet or an undertow. It had always been there. Until now I'd taken a perverse kind of pleasure in resisting it. Suddenly I was so tired, and He was so ready to pull me in where I belonged, where I've always belonged...

Then I remembered things Carmen had said, to me and to others. I was forced to realize that every objection I could bring up she'd already answered.

"I've been ransomed by the death of Christ."

"That's very nice, but I'm a little too far gone."

"All you need is Jesus in your heart."

"I can't do it!"

"He'll give you everything you need."

"Something as good as that can't be for someone like me."

"It's for everybody, but you have to take it."

"Forget it. I wouldn't even know how to take it."

"You only need to ask Him.

"You only need to ask Him.

"You only need..."

It was all piling up on me. A mother's love, the courage of a girl way out of her depth, a mother's hope, half-buried memories and a stunning realization that tragedy doesn't affect reality; pain doesn't change truth. All these years, I'd been lying to myself because of pain, and suddenly I was backed into a corner. I couldn't tell if it was against my will or if I was yielding to it. But whichever it was, I was flooded, overwhelmed, and forced to acknowledge...the Truth.

"ALL RIGHT!" I'm not sure whether I actually yelled it or not. Suddenly the walls around my heart; that empty, sea-shell thing within me that I'd locked in a box to keep from getting hurt any more...those walls I'd built with such bitter and angry resolve ...those walls that continually sparked a war between my will and my loneliness...those walls exploded. I was exposed, naked, shaking, alone and sinful. I was dirty, guilty, soiled and inexcusable. I was examined, judged, found guilty and condemned.

Suddenly there was only one way out; one way to be who and what I was supposed to be; one way to remove the past foolishness and start over. I knew what it was. My mother had told me so many years ago...and Carmen had told Olga. My heart reached and groped. I grasped it, held on, and clung to it like I was drowning.

I was on my knees, shaking and sobbing, saying, "Jesus...oh, Jesus...You know my life's been a...a sham, and I'm not really happy with what I...I've become. Worse than that: You're not happy with it. M...my whole adult life has been...lies...and violence.

"There's not much about me You could use, but I've heard You're a miracle-Worker...so I'll trust You to make me something I'm not. Take what's left of my life and turn it into something You can be pleased with."

I would have said a lot more, but suddenly Carmen and I weren't alone anymore. The door opened quietly, almost silently, and snapped me back into my conditioned responses. I jumped up, turned and froze.

# Chapter 13

A tall, thin, familiar figure stepped inside, pistol in hand. He saw me and smiled. It was almost friendly...the way a wolf is friendly with a lamb. "William Donley, I believe? Mr. Lubenkoff sends his regards."

"You were his next appointment," I guessed, going over what I remembered about this guy.

He nodded. "You cover your tracks well, sir. Only another professional could have found you."

Shifting my feet, closing the distance between us carefully, I said, "I was found by the mercenary of the year."

He knew I meant him and chose to ignore the sarcasm. He tilted his head slightly, as if acknowledging a compliment.

Talk, Donley. Get him off balance if you can. Try to keep him from getting to the point until you're ready.

"We almost met about a year ago, didn't we?"

"Yes, in Saudi Arabia. I hoped you thought I had died in that oil refinery explosion."

I waved that away, to get him used to seeing me moving. "Oh, no! I read your file in Washington recently. Let's see...we picked you up in Turkey a few months later and trailed you right into the Soviet Union. What's your name these days... Vladimir something?"

"Ninshka," he obliged.

I smirked. Any little de-valuing technique might work in the clinches. "Yeah, Ninshka." I switched tactics, hoping to get him off balance. "I wouldn't have thought this little matter would have been big enough for your attention."

He shrugged eloquently. "It's an amusing little diversion; nothing more. Although Dr. Gonsalo has yet to pay for his education."

It was my turn to shrug. "Tell him that."

He glared at me. The veneer melted away and a hardness came over him. "I intend to."

Some people have unusual amusements.

Carmen had stirred at the mention of her father, and now she looked up sleepily. "Who...? Wha...?"

Ninshka moved his gun just enough to cover us both. "Ah. Hello, my dear. Forgive me for disturbing your sleep. You will need all you can get. I'm afraid your new quarters will not be very comfortable."

No, they won't, will they? They had to treat her well before or risk an international incident. Now, the United States believed I'd gotten her out. They would say that, and my government would have to accept it. Then they'd put her in a dungeon designed to make her confess to everything from murder to bad breath. They'd break her will and her morals, make her a compliant zombie and send her to the troops in Siberia or someplace.

Her eyes got big. "Oh, no! We've been caught!"

I had to correct that statement. "Not 'caught', Carmen. Just found. There's a difference."

Ninshka chuckled. "Always the optimist, eh? But let us not be foolish, Mr. Donley. I am sure you are aware that I cannot allow you to leave."

That was all for Carmen's sake. We both knew I was bored listening to all this obvious melodrama.

I was content to let him gloat. I was waiting for the right kind of opening, making little jerky movements like I was nervous. The fact that I was moving in small ways would soon stop getting his attention...or so I hoped. It was old ploy, but it still sometimes worked.

We heard it together: the whirring of the helicopter blades. I let my left hand twitch and draw his attention. He was divided between that and the company we were getting.

I lashed out with my right foot and caught his gun hand with a surprisingly jarring impact. The gun was flying across the room before he could react.

I grabbed his empty hand and the armpit, yelling, "Go, Carmen!" Then I sent him over my shoulder. When his eyes finally focused he was staring at the Beretta's barrel.

What a bonus! Bringing Carmen back would mean a successful assignment, but getting rid of this turkey would be worth at least the long-overdue vacation. Allied agents would be grateful to me for years.

Carmen's words about people dying without Christ assaulted me. Could I really send this guy into eternity...knowing he had no hope?

I had never let an enemy walk away from me before. Some did, but it wasn't because I'd chosen to let them go. That was just the way it was done in this business.

But then I could see Carmen standing over Nadia's body, accusing me and saying, "How can she get saved now?"

Finally, with a groan that seemed more far eloquent than all the snappy remarks I'd ever made, I swung the Beretta. It connected just over his left ear and he went limp.

I looked up. I didn't realize I was speaking out loud when I said, "He's still alive, okay? Now he has a chance to get saved!"

I turned and saw Carmen in the doorway. She'd seen the whole thing, and the look on her face was ecstatic. "You...you..."

That helicopter couldn't wait forever.

"Yeah, yeah, right!" I yelled, "Let's go!"

# *Part 2:*

## THE CHASE DISPATCH

# *Chapter 1*

I watched the receding Bulgarian landscape as the helicopter took off, trying to avoid the feeling that my life was ending.

Down in those woods, already invisible under the trees, was a shack containing the first enemy I'd ever purposely left alive, and the insecurities I'd killed a thousand times rose up and roared within me.

Besides that, Carmen was more excited about the fact that I hadn't killed when I could have--and what it meant to her--than the fact that I had just rescued her.

"Are you serious?" she panted, grabbing my arm. "Did you really get saved?" She had to yell to be heard over the loud "whup-whup" of the helicopter's rotors.

Her question made me uncomfortable. I didn't want to talk about it; not yet. There were still too many unanswered questions.

*Yes, Carmen. I got saved. I gave my life to Jesus and asked Him to change it. Now I suddenly don't know where my life is going.*

Espionage and assassination have no place in this kind of life--I know that much. But it's the only thing I've ever been good at. Besides, I've got enemies all over the globe who'd love to know that I'm not dangerous anymore.

*Yes, Carmen, I got saved. But what am I going to do now?*

All I could say was, "Shh. This will all be over soon, and you'll be back with your dad. You've been angry with me almost since I showed up. Stay that way; it'll be healthier in the long run."

"But..."

I held up my hand and locked her eyes for a moment. What she saw changed her mind about speaking. I could practically read her thoughts: "Oh, I think I get it. You might be saved, but you're still Bill Donley, the man who kills people. God's miracles are not the same as fairy-tale magic; there's no 'presto-change-o' here. You still need to walk some things through...assuming anything really happened, after all."

It must have been something like that. She finally looked down and turned to her window, getting interested in the scenery.

That suited me fine. I wasn't feeling very talkative, myself.

# *Chapter 2*

We saw the cars with the crowd around them and it felt like Carmen's breathing just started. Relief swept over me. The uncomfortable ride was over. I knew she was confused and a little resentful because I didn't want to gush about religious experiences with her. But I couldn't, and that would have to be that.

Then she ruined it by turning to me with a smile. "Soon this will be over. You'll meet my father, we can relax and then we'll be able to talk. You've started a brand-new life. I'd like to see you start it right."

I managed a weak smile and looked away again. Oh, well.

The pilot shouted over his shoulder, "I'm going to have to take right off again. When I land, jump and run. Don't stop until you're in the cars."

We felt the bump and the door was flung open. Carmen thought I was being polite when I let her jump out ahead of me. I would have insisted. I didn't want her to see what I was about to do.

I was right behind her, watching her pick up speed as she ran toward the two cars with three agents around them.

I saw something else. Off to the left, there was a little green Volkswagen. I'd seen a lot of little cars lately. The driver, standing next to the car, caught my glance and got in. I heard the engine start. Carmen's mind was too full of her father and her freedom to hear much of anything.

I changed my course and put on speed, trying to keep my ears closed.

At one point I almost thought I heard her calling me, but I couldn't turn around. I was almost at the car when it started rolling. I had to take a flying leap, and I banged my shin, but I managed to slip into the passenger seat and slam the door as it went into second gear.

By the time I was settled enough to look into the rear-view mirror, they were out of sight.

"Hey!" the driver said, "Earth to Donley. The girl's gonna be okay, man. Your job's over."

I turned my head to look at him for the first time. The handsome, swarthy, ear-to-ear grin belonged to my associate, the Greek station head Costas Angropoulos. We'd worked together before.

"Oh. Sorry, Costas. How's it going over here?"

"Pretty good, man. How 'bout you? You okay? You didn't fall for that girl or nothin', did you?"

That was a good question, though I didn't want to admit it.

I'm afraid...I'm really afraid...that I have. That's why I'm glad you were here, Costas. I hope I can get her out of my head when I'm so far away I can't look at her anymore.

"Naw, nothing like that. She's just...gonna be mad at me, that's all."

He laughed. "Love 'em and leave 'em, huh? That's the way I like it. The only way to go, man."

"It's not like that!" I snapped.

"Huh? You sure you okay?"

"Sorry again. I guess I'm just tired."

"I guess so! I was just thinkin' about those two girls we worked with last summer. Lots of fun and no hard feelings. Remember, Bill?"

Yes, I remembered. We spent a week acting like barnyard animals in heat, then shook hands and went our separate ways. Thinking about it now made me feel like I needed a shower.

"Don't mind me," I said. "Anything to report?"

He relaxed, but the grin disappeared. "Chase wants a verbal report from you. You're booked on the next non-stop from Athens to Washington. All I gotta do is get you to the airport."

"Right away?"

"Yep. She's in a hurry to see you, I guess."

"She's in a hurry, huh?" I muttered.

He laughed again. Complaining, especially about the job, was something he enjoyed. "No peace for the wicked, huh?"

"I guess not," I said, wearily.

Costas got serious again. "But it ain't right, Bill. You haven't had a real break in a long time. That ain't fair, you know?"

"Well, nobody ever said it would be," I commented.

But inside I was steaming.

Oh, no, Chase. You're not going to push my vacation back again. No matter what's breaking loose and no matter where, you just can't afford to use me this time. You'll have to find somebody else.

# Chapter 3

There's a kind of unconscious watchfulness that people in my line of work tend to develop. It's called many things: a sixth sense, a hunch, or something even sillier. It's actually a noticing of minor irregularities as they begin to form a pattern that finally surfaces in our minds as something like, "I feel like someone's watching me," or "Something's wrong here."

Well, there are genuine paranoiacs out there. I'm talking about those of us who aren't (I hope) paranoid.

Anyway, when that happens, we have a choice of games to play. Which one we choose depends on the circumstances.

One is "Lose the Watcher". Crossing against the light, catching a train as the doors are closing, and the old "crowded elevator going up and back staircase down" routine are some of the ways to play that one.

Another, and more desirable, game is "Catch the Watcher". This is basically done with the "turn a corner and duck into a store" routine, so you can see who panics and looks around for you frantically.

You can also go into a phone booth (hard to find these days, I admit) or a bathroom and stay in it until the watcher gets impatient and does something that gives him away.

If you handle it well from there, the watcher can become an unwilling source of all kinds of useful information.

Of course, none of those games can be effectively played in an airplane over the Atlantic Ocean.

I tried to play the game anyway (that's right, I had that feeling) by frequent trips to the men's room and the flight attendants' station to ask for special favors. I succeeded in becoming an annoyance, but not much else.

There was a movie being shown, about victimized women and worthless men. I tried putting on the headset, but the music made me uncomfortable, no matter what kind it was. Finally, I settled on a news channel. There was no mention of Carmen, Dr. Gonsalo or the Romanian escapade, but I wasn't expecting to hear anything about that anyway.

During the last hour of the flight I tried to rehearse what I would say to Chase. Every time I thought it through it came out differently.

When the announcement came to fasten our seat belts, I decided to simply give a very complete report, followed by a demand for that vacation.

# Chapter 4

Chase glared across her desk at me, half in annoyance and half in disbelief. "So," she said, letting out a sigh. "What are you going to do now?"

Yeah, that's the big question, isn't it? What exactly am I going to do now? Become a preacher? That almost makes me laugh. I could never take myself seriously in that role. Continue in this business? Far too many inconsistencies, but I'm not ready to admit that to you. Open a grocery store or something? That's something else I can't picture myself doing. You've touched the question my whole future rests on, Chase: what am I going to do now?

"I'm not sure," I said. "I'll need some time."

"Time? For what?" she snapped. This was unusual coming from her. She was normally crisp and businesslike, with occasional lapses into informality. But this short-fused approach was new.

"To decide," I said, more forcefully than I really had a right to. "Anyway, my vacation is long overdue, if you know what I mean. It's the ideal opportunity to figure things out."

The glare got worse. She started tapping the desk with her pen, then bit her lip and looked away.

I knew what that meant.

I can see it, Chase. I was right about your big rush to get me back here. You just confirmed it. You were going to push that vacation back again, weren't you? You have another "emergency" assignment waiting for me, and you had your conciliatory pep talk all worked out, before I ruined it all with my report.

But I don't have any apologies or compromises, Chase. You'll just have to find someone else to handle this "emergency" for you.

"So, I can give you your vacation and wind up having you quit on me, is that it?" she said.

That was exactly what I expected to happen, but I just nodded and shrugged. "That might happen, yes."

She looked off into the distance again. Without looking at me, she said, "And if I don't let you take your vacation right now?"

It was my turn to sigh. "Then I'll have to resign right now. I really need to do this, Chase. I don't expect you to understand why, and I don't think I can explain any better than I already have, but it is necessary."

A different kind of annoyance flashed across her face this time. "I understand more than you seem to think I do," she muttered, with some reluctance. She chewed her lip, sighed and stared at the wall again for what felt like several minutes.

I kept my mouth shut, letting her fight it out on her own.

Finally, she made up her mind. Her eyes bored into mine as she gave me the ultimatum. "One week, Bill. I need you back in that seat telling me where we stand with each other in exactly one week."

She picked up her pen and started writing furiously. I'd been dismissed.

# *Chapter 5*

Going home for me is a risky business, but I've been doing it so long it's just my routine now.

My block is nothing but apartment buildings. They're all eleven stories high, and anonymously identical. I often get out of the cab on the corner, walk to the building next to mine and enter. Behind the buildings are adjoining courtyards with high wooden fences and locked doors between them. A few generous gifts had bought me the privilege of being the only tenant with keys to these doors. After stepping into my own backyard I simply go inside and upstairs.

At the door, I checked all the little telltale signs to make sure I didn't have unexpected company. Then, three locks and a light switch later, I was looking around my small home.

My apartment is one of the dustiest, loneliest places I know. That's probably because I'm hardly ever there myself. It's more like an expensive display of the furniture I hoped to use when I resigned or retired from the Agency. This kind of work is like sports: retirement comes early...when it comes.

The kitchen had white walls, a table and four chairs, though I never used more than one at a time. I also used the coffee maker, but almost nothing else. The beige living room contained a couch that I never used and a recliner that I always used. In fact, that was where I wound up sleeping most nights. The bedroom had my parents' double bed, which I hardly ever used, and bureau filled with socks, underwear, forgotten mementos, etc. Home, sweet storage facility.

I took enough time to shave, shower and change clothes before rummaging around in my bureau for what I needed.

It took twenty minutes and the beginnings of an anxious sweat to find it: a claim ticket for a storage company in New York City. My mother's belongings were there. I'd put it all away when I joined the Army, so long ago. I hadn't touched it since then. I'd hardly thought about it. I just kept paying the bill, and the one time I'd removed some furniture for this place. Now there was something up there I wanted. This would come first.

Filling up a suitcase for the sake of respectability, I triple-locked the apartment and left the building. I had no sense of being followed. That might have been because I was getting more and more preoccupied.

# *Chapter 6*

I looked out the window of the motel room at the mom-and-pop shops across Flatbush Avenue and chuckled. After that remark I'd made to Chase about going to Brooklyn on my vacation, that's exactly where I wound up. I'd have to watch my jokes in the future.

I'd spent the whole day...between phone calls and meals, that is...fighting with myself about Carmen. She was probably home by now, which meant she was right here in Brooklyn somewhere. The phone book only had eleven Gonsalos listed, and only two Emilios, so I didn't think it would take long to find her and make contact. Still, I'd agonized over it until now.

The trunk from the storage-company had just been delivered. I turned back to it and opened the lid. A flood of memories swept over me as I saw my mother's belongings, hidden away for the past ten years.

I gave myself about half an hour to rummage through the things I'd kept until the government had come along. Finally, on the bottom and in a corner, I found what I wanted.

My mother's Bible.

And I remembered. She used to read to me out of it when I was too young to understand the Elizabethan English. Then she would tell me about it in her own words. After she died I rejected her God. I still admired David and Joshua and others like them. I think my favorite was Samson, the violent womanizer.

I could hardly build on that kind of background now. I needed new references and even new memories.

I went to the bed and stretched out on top of the covers, head propped on two pillows and the Book open on my chest.

Starting at the beginning, I leafed my way through, finding the things she had underlined and circled. Some of it made no sense to me at all, but other parts reached me. Some passages I read over and over, trying to grasp what she'd gotten out of them. Others made me stare out the window at the sky, just considering the magnitude of it all. Then there were those parts that made me keep turning the pages. Things I could tell I wasn't ready for yet.

When I got to the New Testament, I had to slow down the reading and try to figure out what was going on. I had always thought it was just a Life of Christ. When He was already dead and risen at the end of Matthew, and the whole story seemed to start over again three more times, I almost put it down and left it. But something kept calling me, almost pulling me, through the Book.

It only took that afternoon and evening to get through the Book like that. Night had fallen and I needed to sleep.

I don't quite remember getting ready for bed, but soon I was under the covers, my mind somewhere else with a dark Cuban girl with bright eyes.

Now I begin to understand you, Carmen. If the bits and pieces of this Book I've seen are anything like the rest of it, then it's worth whatever the risk to get it into as many hands as possible. Perhaps that's what I ought to do now? I've got contacts in almost every country, especially behind the Iron Curtain. This Bible smuggling may just be where my own future lies.

My future...are you a part of that future, Carmen? I'm beginning to hope so. But that brings on another question: how much of this Christianity is really a subconscious attempt to become more acceptable to you? I'll have to know that before I try to contact you.

Somewhere in those reflections, I dropped out and sleep took over.

# *Chapter 7*

Suddenly I was awake. The room was dark and silent, and everything seemed still.

But something had happened; something had triggered that self-preservation within me; some little whisper that didn't fit brought me back to full wakefulness. This reflex was conditioned into me. It had saved my life too many times to ignore, and I knew what it meant.

I wasn't alone in the room.

Now it was a waiting game, and I had the advantage. I knew he was there, but he thought I was asleep. All I had to do was lie there, be very patient, listen, and pay close attention...

From my left, the slightest sound reached me. A shuffling, like weight being shifted and a foot being moved just a fraction...

Now I had an idea of where he was. I waited until I heard something again. My visitor could not concentrate totally on me and move around in a dark, unfamiliar room at the same time.

My arms and legs worked together to push me into the air. I was reaching for him before my feet hit the floor. I had him almost before he could move.

My left hand grabbed his throat and pushed him back against the wall, squeezing at the same time.

My right hand pumped twice, hard, into his solar plexus.

Then I let him go suddenly and watched him fall forward.

There was time to step over to the wall switch and turn the light on.

I returned to him, put my foot on the small of his back and checked all of his pockets. If he tried to move, I might accidentally break his spine. He knew this, and kept still.

I was actually surprised to find a wallet in his hip pocket. There was even a DC driver's license in it.

"Well, Mr. Jeffrey Logern," I said, "you've come a long way from home to do your breaking and entering."

"I...I thought you...changed," he gasped. "I thought...you got...religion or something."

On top of ruining a perfectly good night's sleep, now he had to go and make me feel guilty. I was angry with him, and that bothered me, too.

"Don't play for time," I said, putting some weight on my foot. "Who sent you and what's your errand?"

That changed the atmosphere. He seemed to remember something and fear became almost a presence in the room with us.

"It's your boss."

"Chase?"

"Whatever."

"What about her?"

He started to squirm. "I can talk better standing up."

"You're doing fine where you are. What about Chase?"

"She's missing."

Missing? She was supposed to have round-the-clock bodyguards watching her. The knowledge she carried between her ears could neutralize this country's interests on almost every continent, and outrage a hypocritical public. Even the officials who were trying to disband our organization would want her protected. This just didn't make sense.

"How long?"

"Since a little after noon. All leaves canceled. You're on assignment."

"I work for Chase, Logern. Nobody else has authority to put me on an assignment."

"Not even the Secretary of Defense?"

"That's easy to say, but I don't see any documentation."

"Don't talk like an idiot, Donley."

Once upon a time I'd have broken his arm for that. Not because I was particularly offended, but to maintain my mystique in the intelligence "community", as it were. I wasn't used to taking abuse from people who broke into my room, but I swallowed it and said, "I'm still not convinced, and you're still an intruder."

There was a hesitation. Finally, he sighed and said, "I'm authorized to give you a phone number."

"So you can knock me out and get away while I listen to Dial-A-Joke? Forget it, Logern."

Another sigh. "If you don't want to call the number, there's nothing else I can say or do."

Well, there it was. If it really was all he had, I could take it or leave it, but I couldn't expect any more out of him...except one thing. "You could have called me on the phone and given me the number. You knew this was my room. Why the cloak and dagger melodrama?"

"My instructions specified face-to-face."

I was sure he didn't want to tell me the rest of it. Surprising the assassin in his bed would be a big plus on his resume and reputation.

Quickly, I took my foot off his back and put my hands under his armpits, lifting. He cooperated, pushing up and getting his feet under him.

Before he could completely get his balance I pushed him toward the desk by the window with the telephone on it.

"You dial the number," I said, "and I'll talk to the nice gentleman."

He sat down and grinned maliciously. "Aren't you going to warn me not to try anything?"

I grinned back. "I don't really think I have to."

That wasn't a boast, and he knew it. He started to punch the numbers, saying, "What you did in Cairo last year is well known in my circles, Donley."

Sure, it's well known. That was the CIA operative who didn't like my attitude when I didn't believe who he was. He tried to put me in my place. But I was playing hardball, and he hadn't convinced me that my life wasn't on the line. He unplugged the phone and threw it at me, just to put himself at an advantage. I caught it and he reached for his gun. So I kicked the gun out of his hand and strangled him with the telephone cord.

That caused heavy friction between agencies, and I knew I could never expect a lot of help from CIA personnel in the future.

But Chase had stood by me then.

I wasn't proud of that episode anymore, but that one fact stood out. Chase had stood by me. It seemed that now it was my turn to stand by her.

Logern handed the receiver to me. It was still ringing. Then there was a click and a familiar voice said, "Mr. Donley?"

"Yes, sir?" I said, playing it out.

"I want to confirm and expand what you've just heard. Your superior, the head of your agency, left her office at twelve hundred hours and took an official car to the shopping district. She entered a department store at twelve-twenty and has not been seen since."

"Excuse me, sir."

"Yes, what is it?" I had interrupted his recital, and he was slightly annoyed with me.

"I don't mean to be insubordinate, but I'm several hundred miles away now, in a motel room, listening to a disembodied voice that claims to be the Secretary of Defense. I admit it sounds like the right voice, but that's easily faked. Just how do I know who I'm speaking to?"

"Acknowledged, Mr. Donley. You're correct, of course. This assignment is 'Jean Juares, Heracles'. Do you understand now?"

Jean Juares, the French socialist whose assassination was one of the lesser-known triggers of the First World War. Heracles, the classical hero who tried to get out of fighting in the Trojan War, but couldn't. Only five people outside our agency knew that code, and the Secretary of Defense was one of them. "Jean Juares" meant the absolute highest priority; the only alternative was a real possibility of global war. "Heracles" meant I had no choice; refusing this assignment would be considered an act of treason.

"I understand, sir."

"Needless to say, I won't be able to give any official recognition to this matter. I will only spell it out this once, and then you'll be on your own. We will not, repeat will not, be communicating again until this is over."

"Yes, sir."

"No one has communicated with us, so we have no reason to believe she's being held for ransom; at least, not yet. The only other reason we can think of is extraction: she was abducted for the information she carries."

I could think of a few other reasons, but I kept them to myself. Besides, there was something more important on my mind. "Excuse me, sir."

"What?" He was getting downright testy with me now.

"I don't understand how this could have happened the way you said it did, if her bodyguards were on duty."

"Her bodyguards were indeed on duty. It seems that she purposely eluded them. And that brings me to the second half of my instructions for you."

I wasn't sure how much more there could be. All I said was the usual, "Yes, sir?"

"If you find her, and for any reason she is unwilling to cooperate with you, dispatch will be necessary."

Dispatch. He was ordering me to kill her.

# Chapter 8

I put the receiver down slowly, staring at Logern.

"You see?" he challenged. "You satisfied now?"

Turning away from him to stare out the window, I said, "Do you have anything to add to that?"

"No, that's it. The whole idea was to get you to call."

"It was a stupid idea. It almost got you killed, and I could have been incarcerated. Tell them that for me when you get back. Well, mission accomplished. Try to do it in a less suicidal way next time. Go on home, Logern."

He didn't like being dismissed that way. However, he was too happy at the thought of getting away at all to protest much.

Soon I was alone again in that anonymous room, with my mother's trunk, my mother's Bible, and no vacation.

I decided I might as well start this unwanted assignment fed and rested, so I called the desk to request a wake-up call and tumbled back into bed.

The cab driver didn't shut up once, all the way to LaGuardia Airport. His anger at corruption in government continued from the Brooklyn-Queens Expressway to the slightly faster-moving Long Island Expressway. When he turned onto the Van Wyck Expressway he was giving me his answers to the problem. "They oughta take every one o' those bums," he said, "and put 'em on a boat. Then they oughta send the boat into shark-infested waters and punch a hole in it."

"Well, that ought to get rid of those politicians," I conceded, hoping he'd get my point.

"It sure would!" he said, missing my point. "I'd like to be there, just to see it!" Now he was talking like it really would happen.

*And people think I'm dangerous!* I thought.

He surprised me when he pulled up in front of the terminal by getting my suitcase out of the trunk for me.

I left him a good tip...it was, after all, an unusually fast ride...and stepped through the electric eye doors.

Before I went ten steps I had them spotted. There were three of them, pretending they didn't see me and didn't care. I'd been trained the same way, and I knew what to look for.

*Lord, what am I doing here? How do I handle this without either getting killed or compromising You?*

I decided to let my conditioning take over, hoping I could control it in the clinches.

Without breaking stride, I headed toward the escalator down to the baggage claim area. All the while, I hoped they wouldn't notice the inconsistency of it.

At the bottom, I slipped to the right and put the suitcase down for some quick-change moves.

Pulling off my jacket, I grabbed my suitcase and slipped back through to the claims area, jumping off and stooping my shoulders. Posture and deformity are all that most people notice about strangers, especially when under pressure.

A group was heading for the escalator from another direction, chattering happily. I attached myself to the family reunion with a vacant smile. They thought I was a little strange. Anyone else would have thought I was part of the group. The watchers were looking for a single man. They wouldn't waste time studying a whole family.

I hoped.

How could people know I'm on assignment already? It was only five hours ago when I'd hung up the phone. Could Logern have broken and told someone? No, that means that somebody was already interested in my activities.

Who, then? The Secretary of Defense was almost paranoid about security here. Otherwise, he'd have had some assistant's assistant talk to me. I was sure he was on a secured cell phone in an empty plaza when we'd talked. That phone was now at the bottom of the Potomac.

That only left the unknown party involved in Chase's disappearance. Elementary perhaps. Sometimes these cases get so convoluted I need to keep reminding myself who's who.

I was suddenly aware of a comforting weight in my jacket pocket. My instinct was to think it was a gun, but I knew it was the pocket-sized Bible I'd bought that morning.

The plane ride was just a short hop, but I still managed to divide my time between reading in the New Testament and trying to make some kind of sense out of the LaGuardia incident.

Why so soon? I didn't know anything; I wasn't sure I'd get to the first move without being checkmated by my own people. Could there be a third group? This one looking for Chase for their own reasons and hoping I'd let them follow me around? On the other hand, why would the people who had her want to tail me so early in the game?

I had to stop when I realized I didn't know enough to even think properly about things yet. My finger was still on the place where I'd stopped reading. I looked at the next verse, which was the beginning of a whole new chapter:

*"Let not your heart be troubled; Ye believe in God, believe also in Me."*

This was Jesus speaking, and it reached me in ways I couldn't understand.

*"Let not your heart be troubled."*

It was ironic. Before I committed my life to Jesus Christ, these assignments had never troubled me. Now suddenly I needed assurance and comfort.

I spent the rest of the trip staring at clouds, trying to figure out why I was so determined to make this commitment work. The question came up again. Was it just for Carmen, or was it more than that? I thought I could put that one to rest. If this was just an act for her benefit, I wouldn't have avoided making contact when I was in Brooklyn.

# Chapter 9

It was a nondescript office building, almost invisible in its anonymity. There were teams of guards around it day and night, but they also blended in with the surroundings. Inside, an intricate security system made the employees feel safe.

Until they left.

Now it was my job to violate that same security...and on its own behalf. I could hear myself, if caught, trying to answer questions:

"Why did you violate the security of your agency?"

"So it could stay secure."

"What does that mean?"

"I can't tell you."

"Why not?"

"I'm not sure I know myself. Besides, telling you would violate that security."

I entered the building with an attitude of preoccupation. Sometimes I was playful, but usually I was like this. Just a businessman, going to work. The security team was there, as several people entered and left around me. This gave the impression that normal business was conducted there, and made it harder for an observer to zero in on the person who was really entering or leaving.

In the lobby I continued toward the elevators, aware of the unblinking light lenses glaring at me and trying to remember how I normally acted when I didn't have to think about it.

And inside I wanted to scream at them all, "Don't any of you understand? Haven't you heard? I can't be a deceiver anymore, and I don't want to be! Why couldn't you just leave me alone?"

Well, I hadn't actually lied to anybody yet. There was a little comfort in that.

Then I was at the door to the office. All surveillance would stop as I entered. Security personnel didn't have to know what was spoken about in this room. Most of the information was on a strictly "need to know" basis.

Inside the room with the door shut behind me, I knew I had a free hand...until I found what I wanted.

It took just under an hour to find it. Under the hollow of Chase's desk, where her feet would normally be, a tile was loose.

That's the trouble with electronic security, I thought, people depend on it. When there are cameras and microphones hidden all over the place, we don't try very hard to hide our valuables. All a good thief has to do is get past the gadgets and he's got it made.

Almost.

I knew all the alarms would be going off as soon as I lifted that tile. It would be a matter of seconds before security guards would be keeping me company. If there was a combination lock under this tile, the assignment might well be over before it even started.

It seemed that there was only one thing to do. I leaned back and looked up at the blank, white ceiling. "God," I said, out loud, "I'm not even sure I have a right to ask You for help in something like this...but an awful lot is depending on how this works out. So...so, I need to go for it, and I'll be counting on You, more than any skills I have." Then I remembered how Carmen ended her prayers, and said, "In Jesus' Name, Amen."

It sounded strange, unspiritual and embarrassing to my own ears, but I felt a little better, anyway. After wiping my hands on my pants, I poised over the tile and counted to three. Then I pulled it carefully aside with my left hand and put it down gently as my right started to reach inside.

I nearly gave the whole thing up right then. There was a combination lock. The seconds were ticking. I took a chance and grabbed the handle anyway. It opened easily.

*Congratulations, Chase. Your own carelessness is working with you this time. Or was it carelessness? Did you leave it like this for me?*

There was only one sheet of paper inside, which I pocketed. Then I replaced the door, replaced the tile, and stood up. I looked at my watch as I stepped away from the desk. As the footsteps approached I stood like a statue. The door opened and someone yelled, "Freeze!"

"It took you fifteen seconds to get here," I said. "In that time I could have killed two people, grabbed a handful of top-secret documents off that desk, and escaped out the window to a waiting helicopter with a rope for me."

I looked up. There were two of them, guns trained on me. They didn't quite believe me yet, my confidence made them hesitate. Besides, an enemy wouldn't hang around to criticize their response.

"I did that once," I went on, "in South America. It's in the files, and you guys are supposed to be aware of it. Is that what happened to Chase? Is all this garbage about how she avoided you just a big cover-up for your inefficiency? What were you two doing that it took so long to get here when the alarm went off?"

Their lowered guns were still pointed in my general direction. Their faces reflected a quick series of emotions as I talked, and settled on fear.

I stepped back behind the desk and sat, indicating the two chairs facing it. "You two need to sit down," I said. "I have a lot of questions."

# *Chapter 10*

"First," I said, "your names. We'll settle for last names until more is required." I looked at them and waited.

One of them recognized me. He relaxed just enough to say, "My name is Slajewski." They're supposed to be able to recognize those who belong in the building.

I turned my eyes to the other, who promptly spouted, "Janssen."

I repeated my offer to sit and they took me up on it. When they were seated I said, "You were on duty yesterday morning, correct?"

They nodded.

"Tell me about it. In your own words."

Janssen looked exasperated. He would have told the same story more times than he could remember in the last twenty-four hours. Here I was pushing my weight around and saying, "Play it again, Sam."

Slajewski answered, with a stoically patient look on his face. "The subject signed in at zero eight hundred hours, using the all-clear. That's her voice-print saying the name 'Ms. Pursue'." He made a grimace of distaste when he said that. It was an obvious clue, and a clumsy pun. She should have come up with a better code. I agreed with him. "She came directly to this office and remained until twelve hundred hours. Then she left, without signing herself out. This was irregular, so Janssen was assigned to follow her."

Janssen was about to take over when I held up my hand and addressed Slajewski. "How come I don't have to sign in and out like that?"

"Several different government agencies have their headquarters in this building. They're not all in the intelligence community. The field agents are monitored by computer as they come and go. They're never around for more than a few hours at a time. Our primary responsibility is for the people who are here all day."

"Okay, I get it. Now, Janssen, what happened after she left?"

He looked uncomfortable, but picked up the narrative. "There was an eighty-three Olds waiting for her. It had tinted windows. I don't like 'em. Makes me think something's going on inside the car. Anyway, she got in the back seat and the car took off. I got into a vehicle and stayed two or three cars behind until she left the vehicle at Bartholomew and Thomas, the department store. I sent the driver in pursuit of the car and tried to stay with the subject."

"Tried?"

"Well...the sidewalk was crowded. By the time I was inside the doors, she was gone. I staked out the store for the next two hours. I never saw her again."

"What about the car?"

He shook his head. "Our man was trapped in a traffic jam."

I sighed. "Oh, well." Then I got up. They did the same. We left the office together. As we waited for the elevator, I said, "Thanks for being so honest. It sounds like you did all you could."

The relief showed on their faces, but they said nothing.

The elevator arrived and we rode down in silence. When the doors opened in the lobby, I left the building without looking back.

# *Chapter 11*

To get back home I used my "C & S Route"...circuitous and surreptitious, if you must know...and was soon riding the elevator. On the way up I fingered the paper impatiently, barely controlling myself until the doors opened on my floor.

I hurried to my apartment. After going through the usual procedure to check for visitors, I let myself in.

Now I could relax and think. I remembered those intimidated guards, sensing their own failure without quite understanding it. I chuckled to myself. Although they worked in "security" for an "intelligence" outfit, they were pretty dim.

One thing was obvious: Chase had disappeared because she'd wanted to. Also, she'd had at least one accomplice, possibly two. The driver of her car might have been the third person.

To make it work, she would have been wearing a wraparound dress, with a low hem and a high neckline. A blouse and culottes on underneath, and a red or blonde wig waiting in the car would be all she needed.

The other accomplice would have been in the back seat of the car with her. This one was a woman, ready to put on Chase's dress and stroll into the store. Chase herself stayed in the car and made for parts unknown. Inside the store, an artistic person could make a change right in front of everyone without attracting attention. Then the female accomplice would have left the store as herself, while all the watchers looked for Chase.

I'd done that a few times myself. I only had to look like I was trying things on, buy a few things and decide to keep wearing them. I'd left stores looking thirty years older and forty pounds heavier than when I'd entered. Chase had been amused at my reports.

Are you amused now, Chase? Are you sitting back somewhere laughing at all of us running around trying to find you? No, I don't think so. I know you too well. There was a good reason for you to do this. I'm afraid I know what it was.

I shook myself. Speculation would be useless until I'd read the paper I'd found in Chase's floor-safe. I fished it out of my pocket and unfolded it.

One look and I laughed. Oh, if only those guards could see this! Taking a deep breath, I settled down to read:

*"Bill,*

*"I'm terribly sorry to do this to you, but it's necessary. I was going to send you straight to the Bahamas on another case when you shocked me like you did.*

*"Don't try to find the people who helped me. They're part-timers who don't know enough to help.*

*"We have a simple, but serious, problem: All our Caribbean interests are being threatened. Word is out that some super-weapon is hidden somewhere, aimed at us.*

*"I couldn't put this one on hold. Cuba and Nicaragua have both fallen to the communists. We can't lose anything else in this hemisphere if we can help it. I've already sent two agents, and they've both disappeared.*

*"Bill, you're the best I've got. I didn't want to violate your conscience until you'd made your decision, but I need you on this case. That's why I'm forcing the Secretary's hand.*

*"Take a flight to Nassau and make the normal contact. The code will be 'Jules Verne'. Find Alfredo Murales. After that, I'll find you."*

There was no signature. It wasn't necessary.

Just then I heard the "click" on my locked front door as it opened.

That wasn't right.

No one had the key to this apartment but me and...uh-oh. The super. All my usual precautions had been taken, of course. Somehow, somebody had found a way around them.

# *Chapter 12*

I didn't bother to grab a weapon. Instead, I jumped behind the door just before it opened and waited to welcome my visitor.

A young, badly frightened black man stepped cautiously into the room. He looked like he wanted to step back out and run.

Before he could move, I stepped up beside him and grabbed his left wrist in both hands. Then I squeezed the bone just above the wrist and rolled it downward, bringing his arm toward me as I stepped away.

He went down so fast his knees bounced off the floor. I put a little pressure on his elbow, just to let him know I could snap it any time I wanted to.

"My arm!" he screamed.

"It's my arm now!" I hissed into his ear. "I'll break it if I want to. You might get it back if I like what I hear. Who sent you and why are you in my apartment?"

His body shuddered, a spasm-like thing that was like fear, but strangely different.

I put a little more pressure on his elbow, and said, "Talk to me. I won't wait forever."

Still shuddering, he blurted a jumble of syllables that meant nothing to me.

"Not so fast, pal," I cut in. "Now let's start over and slow it down, so I can understand. Once again, who sent you and why?"

He twisted and turned, resisting me. Putting still more pressure on his elbow, I heard it snap, but he didn't stop. His face was contorted with sweat, pain and fear. However, his strength was amazing. He threw me against the wall, where I could only stare at him, wondering how he could do that while in such pain.

He spouted some more gibberish, and surprised me by running away from the door, to the window.

It's the fifth floor, I thought, starting after him. I briefly pondered that helicopter-and-rope trick, but this area was too congested. There were too many buildings and too much air traffic for it to work.

The window exploded and I watched him sail out in a shower of glass. By the time I got to the window and looked down, he was almost on the ground. He was falling limply and awkwardly, arms and legs flailing in seemingly impossible directions. He landed with a sickening thud.

The silence of the street was palpable; a ponderous blanket that seemed to weigh everything down. I looked up and down the street. Not a soul. It's hard to believe that could happen on a block with so many residences. I knew it wouldn't last. Any moment now, someone would step outside and see the mangled, broken body sprawled in the street under my broken window.

I ran to the phone and punched in the usual number. Normally I would have reached Chase. This time the extra clicks signaled that the call was re-routed. Finally, a male voice just said, "Yes."

"Jean Juares, Heracles."

"Go on, please."

"I need a cleanup crew on Connecticut Street, North West." I briefly gave him the address and explained the situation, ending with, "I can't stay around. This was not, repeat not, a dispatch. The subject committed suicide when I caught him breaking in."

"Any marks?"

"Bruised wrist, possibly broken elbow. Nothing else from me."

"Okay, Heracles. Get out of there. We'll take care of it."

Now I was Heracles. Amusing, though I found the pagan connection a little disturbing. The man had said to get out, so I got out. I grabbed my toothbrush, wallet and suitcase. After one quick look around I left the way I'd come.

I was off to the sunny Caribbean.

# Chapter 13

The Bahamas. I'd passed through there several times. Only twice had my assignment actually centered on the islands.

Once was to pay back one of Chase's inter-departmental debts. We had to put the skids on a drug-smuggling operation. I'd always considered that kind of job a waste of time and energy. The stuff would come in to the island of Great Abaco by plane, go out by boat and be disbursed in Miami.

Blowing up the first plane was the hardest part. A determined ground crew kept trying to rescue the cargo from the flames. I had to keep cutting them down. I'd let one person survive each time I hit them. I had to hit three planes and two boats before they finally wised up and moved on. Six months later I found out they were back at it again.

Like I said, a waste of time and energy.

The other one was more fun. There was a fat cat who was financing an African coup. I learned that he had a weakness for gambling. The mercenaries in Africa had done most of their dirty work, but wanted their money before they finished. We knew he'd want to play on the night before the payoff, sort of like getting the most out of the money before letting it go. The right kind of pressure on the casino owner gave me access to the baccarat cards and the dealer's confidence. After I'd doctored the cards so they'd be dealt correctly, I had the decks shrink-wrapped to look fresh. Once the game started, it was a matter of playing his emotion until the gambling fever gripped him. A pinch of Demerol in his on-the-house drinks also helped to impair his judgment and weaken his will power.

About two-thirty in the morning, he was wiped out. A well-timed urgent phone call arrived for me. I picked up my winnings, promised to be right back, and took off.

Twelve hours later, the remains of his body washed up on the beach, ruining a few vacations. About a week later, a few newspaper columnists tried to figure out why the guerrillas had suddenly disappeared from the little African nation.

This visit to the islands was different. I didn't know what was going on. The helpless feeling that I was being manipulated came close to infuriating me. That also bothered me, because now I was supposed to be filled with peace and joy and such like.

I was in a plane again, Bible open on my lap. It seemed that there were a lot of demons flying around in those days, latching onto people whenever they could. Jesus and His followers spent a lot of time knocking them around.

Now that gave me something to think about. If that was for real, why wasn't it still happening today?

Or was it? Maybe this was another of those things I never heard because I wasn't listening. Just imagine that kind of power! It didn't seem to be the kind of thing I could use for my own reasons, though. Setting people free from the things appeared to be the only acceptable reason to do it. Still, I wondered if it would come in handy in a job like this. It would be interesting to find out.

My "usual contact" had moved to the island of Great Inagua, the southernmost of the Bahamas. He was called Omar. He lived in a bungalow-type house about ten feet south of Lake Rosa. I'd once asked why he wanted to live by a lake with all the ocean to look at. He'd scowled and said, "When I look at the ocean, man, it don't end. When I look at the lake, I know the other side ain't far away. I like that."

The small plane from Nassau touched down at the primitive airport in Matthew Town. The pilot opened the door. I stepped out, taking a deep breath of the salty air and enjoying the warm breeze. It was a far cry from Romania, and even Washington, for that matter.

As I started to walk away, the pilot called, "Yeah, mon!"

I turned. "Yeah?"

"I seen you readin' dat Bible. You a believer?"

I couldn't help smiling. "Uh, yeah," I said, lamely.

"Well, you be mighty careful, bro. De Holy Ghos', He tell me you gonna need lots o' prayer, mon!"

I stared at him for a long moment, then nodded. "Thanks, uh...thanks for telling me."

He nodded solemnly. "You bet. Hey, what's your name, if you allowed to tell me?"

"Bill Donley," I blurted, realizing that I had no cover identity for this assignment.

"Bill, I tell my pastor 'bout you pretty soon, an' he get de whole church to pray. You like dat?"

"I like it a lot. What church?"

"Gospel Holiness Church, on de nort' side of de island. You come see us when you can, okay?"

"Okay! Thanks again!" I turned, feeling strangely elated, and started toward the taxi stand. I was a mile away before I realized I didn't know the pilot's name.

# *Chapter 14*

The taxi driver nodded smartly and put the car in gear when I told him where I wanted to go. He wasn't the talkative type. That was fine with me. I stared out the window and breathed some more of that clean, salty air. I don't usually get much of it where I'm sent.

Finally, he pulled in front of the house and said, "This is the place, man."

"It sure is!" I said, cheerfully.

The familiar bungalow in that weird shade of green, with the porch across the front, looked deserted. I stepped toward the front door as the engine started behind me. I took a few more steps and heard the car brake to a stop, change gears and start again.

A familiar voice bellowed, "Okay, freeze, turkey!"

I knew it wasn't addressed to me, but I froze anyway. Taking things like that for granted is one way to solve retirement problems.

Then I heard, "Aw c'mon, cousin! You know I didn't mean you!"

That was so unexpected I had to turn around, slowly and carefully.

A muscular black man stood in the policeman's pose: legs spread, both hands holding a .38 at arm's length. He was pointing it at my driver, who was holding a small camera.

The driver was sullen. "No crime to take pictures, man."

"No?" my contact said. "Well, I'm a private person, this is my private property and that's my private friend. People I don't know offend me when they take pictures of my private friends on my private property."

I took the cue and approached the cab. "So what are the pictures for?" I demanded. "I can tell you're not a tourist." He gave me a hostile glare until I said, "Look, tourists don't usually drive their own taxis around." Then I grinned at my benefactor. "How you doin'?" I said to Omar, the black Columbia graduate who'd worked hard to lose his accent and then worked just as hard to get it back again when he'd joined the Agency. I was just as careful to avoid using his name as he'd been to avoid using mine. There was no point in giving the opposition any freebies.

As I approached the cab, the driver got nervous. "Hey, man...it's...it's somethin' I do, y'know? Moonlight."

"Moonlight, huh?" I asked, snatching the camera. "Who you do it for?"

"Uh...freelance."

Omar spat in disgust. "'Freelance'. 'Moonlight'. Man, this dirtbag usin' a lotta words to say nothin'."

"Nothing, nothing," I said, pulling the film cartridge from the camera. "And that's about the quality of the pictures you've got, isn't it?" I tossed the empty camera into the cab, just missing the driver's nose. Leaning on the door, I said, "You go back home and tell your boss I don't like foolishness. If he wants to know something, he can just come over and ask. If I think it's something he should know, I'll tell him myself."

"Now," Omar said, "my friend just talked me outta blowin' you away, so you can just get off my private property, like now!"

That was all he needed. Taking full advantage of the reprieve, he gunned the engine and was racing away in seconds.

Omar put his gun away, grinning. "Okay, Bill!" he said. "Now it's time for Part Two!" He started to run and I followed.

On the other side of his house was a Jeep Renegade. We jumped in and were soon catching up to our friend the photographer. He didn't recognize us. Very calmly, he pulled over and let us pass.

"Lend me your piece," I said to Omar. "I need to finish this."

He pulled out his .38 and passed it over. I leaned out the window and aimed carefully, squeezing the trigger. I felt the recoil and saw the rear left tire blow apart almost simultaneously. Then I turned around in the seat without waiting to see what the driver thought about his new problem.

Omar gave me a strange, questioning look as he turned his CB on. "Kingpin, this is Octopus. Come in, Kingpin. Over."

After three tries, we heard a crackle followed by, "Hey, Octopus Man! Where you been? Everything okay at Rosa?"

"Well, the party's over, I'm late for work, and someone needs a ride home. Send a car, okay?"

I heard a change in Kingpin's voice as he said, "Don' worry 'bout anything, Octopus. You go on to work, man. Everything will be taken care of when you get back home."

"Thanks, Kingpin. Octopus out."

After a few moments I said, "Octopus?"

He grinned, looking very satisfied. "Yeah, man. My hands into so many things, they say I got more than two."

I chuckled as we hit a bump, and held on tighter.

After a hesitation, Omar said, "Bill, tell me somethin'."

"Sure, what?"

"You under deep cover or somethin'? I ain't never seen you let an enemy live when you didn't have to. That just ain't like you, Bill. What's up?"

Well, this had to happen sooner or later...but I still felt a sickly kind of discomfort sweep over me. "Well, uh...I don't dispatch anymore."

Omar's eyes got big. All he said was, "Wha-at?"

At this point we were driving along an almost deserted beach. "Why don't you pull over?" I said. "We can talk for a few minutes."

He didn't say anything, but he pulled the Jeep onto the shoulder of the road and we stepped out. Omar walked next to me in silence, waiting. There were four pleasure boats within sight, out on the water, and a few people getting tans on the beach. Everyone was beyond hearing range.

I kept my eyes moving while I spoke. "My last assignment was in Romania," I began. "I had to rescue a captured Bible smuggler."

"A captured what smuggler?"

"You heard me."

"But...why would somebody want to smuggle something like a Bible? It's not like you can get a lotta cash on a deal like that..."

"That's not true," I interrupted. "On the black market it can bring quite a bit in certain countries. But the thing here is, the Communist Bloc finds Christianity threatening, and it's hard to be a Christian over there. They persecute the Church when outsiders aren't watching, and they regulate the printing and sale of Bibles so it's almost impossible to get one.

"Because of that, some Christian groups in the West do anything they can to get Bibles into these countries. They can print them cheaply, and they get volunteers to take them in. One of the most common methods is...smuggling."

"Okay, so someone got caught smuggling Holy Books into Romania. Why'd they send you, of all people, to the rescue?"

"Her father, a nuclear physicist, was the price of her freedom. The States didn't want to lose him, so they sent me instead."

"And you got her out?"

I nodded, looking at the boats.

"Okay, but..." Then he caught on. "Oh, no! She...she converted you! You...you seen the light, or somethin'."

I nodded again. "Something, yeah."

"Oh, man!" He'd been looking at the water also. Now he slapped his forehead, turned to me, and grabbed my shoulders. "Aw, man! What good you gonna be to me now, huh?"

# Chapter 15

"Nobody wants this assignment less than I do!" I told him, letting the anger out. "Why don't you call the Secretary of Defense and complain? Maybe you'll change his mind and he'll let you take over, okay?"

His expression changed. "The Secky sent you here? Somethin' big must be goin' down for that, man!"

"Jean Juares."

Omar slapped his forehead again. "You mean the Secky send you down here to stop World War Three right after you get religion?"

"Something like that."

He sighed. "Maybe I wake up soon and this ain't happenin'."

"Yeah, maybe."

He threw his hands up in the air. Anyone watching would have thought we were trading boasts and lies. "You might as well let me know what it's about; it can't get no worse."

I was starting to get suspicious, but I gave it to him anyway. "Jules Verne," I said.

The blank stare said everything, but he added, "I tried to read his stuff once, but it was too technical. So what's he got to do with it?"

I let out a sigh, my worst fears confirmed. "That's supposed to be the code, buddy."

"Not by me, it ain't. Bill, what's goin' on here?"

That's what I wanted to know. Chase had given me this code for him and he's never heard of it.

"You mean you don't know what's going on down here?" I said, trying without hope to jog something in his memory. "You weren't expecting me? You're not on assignment?"

He shrugged. "I'm not sure what you mean, 'on assignment'. I'm watchin' the island, man. That's my job. I'm s'posed to help you, or any agent, who comes down. But nobody told me nothin' 'bout no 'Jules Verne'."

"You haven't heard from Chase?"

"Was she s'posed to call me?"

I sighed again. "Omar, she's supposed to be here. I think she was planning a face-to-face briefing with you."

"Well, Bill, it looks like someone very successful don't want that to happen, you know what I'm sayin'?"

About an hour later, we were in Omar's place, facing each other over cups of coffee across his kitchen table.

"So you up against the ol' brick wall this time," he said. "What you gonna do now?"

"Well, I know this sounds crazy, but I don't think I'm up against any wall at all, really."

"You don't? Why not?"

I took a sip and leaned back. "Because they're still trying to stop me."

He nodded thoughtfully, then said, "Who's 'they'?"

I smirked at him. "The bad guys, Omar. Who else would 'they' be?" Then I got serious. "I can't even guess at this point, even if I just believe that note in Chase's office. She just said something about a super-weapon."

Omar got up. "Super-weapon! Man, this is the craziest mess you ever got into. First you get religion, then your boss breaks security and takes off. Then the Secky says you gotta stop World War Three. Now they're into comic book stuff, lookin' for super-weapons!"

I couldn't help grinning. "And it's the same case!"

Omar paced while I sipped, then he turned to me. "We could check all the airports, until we find out which flight she came in on."

I waved the thought away. "She was already anonymous and invisible when she left DC. In fact, she's not even officially here."

"Well, we could talk to independent flyers, and then..."

I thought about that, missing the rest of his suggestion, before shaking my head. "Take too long."

"How 'bout boats?"

"Same."

He sat down then, disgusted and a little angry. "Okay then, Mr. Genius-Man, how 'bout you get some ideas?"

And there it was. It seemed that everywhere I turned lately I found a dead end and frustration. I'd need time to think. I said, "Let's go at it from another direction. Tell me about Alfredo Murales." I hoped that would buy me some time.

He nodded. "Cuban. He's doin' everything he can to stir things up against the U.S. and the local government."

"Any pattern yet?"

"Not yet. We're watchin' him, though." He hesitated. "That's not right. We found one pattern, but it don't make no sense."

"What kind of pattern?"

"He disappears every two weekends. Somethin' to do with his, uh...religion, the reports say."

"Oh. I thought he was a Commie."

"He, uh...he is."

"Wait a minute, Omar. We can't have it both ways. It's one or the other, you know?"

He shrugged. "I know, man. Can't understand it, either. But that's what they're sayin'."

I looked out the window, at the lake. "I wonder if he could have intercepted Chase."

Omar smirked. "She prob'ly intercept him, man! Then he might just turn the tables on her. This dude's never been caught or beat."

"Then how come you know so much about him?"

"'Much'! This ain't nothin'. We got encyclopedias on most agents, whatever countries they're workin' for. We barely got three pages on him. We can't stay on his tail long enough to learn anything."

"Oh, I don't know. Three pages might be enough. For instance, you said he's stirring things up. Like what? What's the last thing he 'stirred up'?"

"Well... Oh, yeah! He had the Haitians up in arms against the local government boys."

I got up. "That's great, we've got a starting point now. Where do these Haitians hang out?"

Omar wasn't ready, though. "They don't really hang out, Bill. They're not s'posed to be here, so they got to keep low profiles, y'know?"

"But I'll bet you know where to find them."

He grinned. "Sure do."

"Let's go."

# *Chapter 16*

We didn't even need the Jeep. As we walked, he chuckled and said, "Sometimes it pays to live on Great Inagua, man. This is the closest island to Haiti, so this is where we find most of 'em."

On a street running parallel to the coast, Omar found what he wanted: a white shingled building with a nicely hand-painted sign in the window saying, "Pirate's Cove".

"Here we are, man."

I stared at it. A bar. Of course it was a bar; where else would we look? I didn't really think we'd find many violent Haitians at the Gospel Holiness Church. So why was I so reluctant to step inside?

"Bill, I been in here a coupla times when I was busted up some, and you were part of my cock-and-bull cover story. The owner knows you...but she don't know what we do, okay?"

"How does she know me?"

"Well, I explained the damage with a fairy tale that had you in it. Just thought you ought to know."

"Yeah, I got that from the first thing you said. I mean, was I a good guy or am I going to get jumped in there?"

He just shook his head and chuckled.

"Thanks a lot," I said.

He led the way inside and I followed, trying to look as though I belonged. I kept my eyes lowered so I wouldn't stare or unconsciously examine anything, but I could sense the "alien among us" change in the atmosphere as I slid onto the stool next to Omar's.

"Hey, Lorna baby, how's it goin'?" he called, and the heavyset barmaid ambled over.

"Hey, sweet thing, how you been?" She glanced at me briefly, then back to Omar.

He read the unspoken question and said, "Oh, I been showin' my friend Bill some things on the island that the tourists never find. I told you about Bill a few times, remember?"

She thought, then brightened. "Oh, yeah!" She turned a toothy smile at me and held out a hand. "Bill, it's good to meet ya! Omar told me about how you saved his life last year. What you drinkin'?"

There it was. I coughed. "Well, uh...I'm driving, Lorna. I'll stick to ginger ale, okay?"

Lorna looked puzzled, but finally shrugged. "That ain't what I expected to hear, man! But whatever you want, you got comin', you hear?"

While she was pouring, Omar kept up his ice breaking. "I thought you'd like him, Lorna. He said he wanted to check out some local color."

She gave out one of the biggest, brightest grins I've ever seen and said, "Well, he sure do need some kinda color, you know what I mean?"

And that did it. The ice was broken. The dozen or so other customers laughed, I laughed, and I was adopted. I was now an honorary "member" of the crowd.

"Where'd you learn that Brooklyn street talk, Lorna?" I asked.

"In Brooklyn, honey. Just wanted you to feel at home." She saw the look on my face and said, "Oh, you hide it well, but not that well. You're from New York, homeboy!"

That brought more laughs.

I leaned back and took a sip of ginger ale, wishing I'd ordered something else... cola, club soda...or something. Well, that much was easy, I thought. Now for the hard part.

Things got more and more natural as we sat there, and I got really sick of ginger ale. Two hours later, the door opened, and four men came in. One was black, the other three Hispanic.

"Well!" Lorna boomed. "If it ain't United Nations Night at the Pirate's Cove tonight!"

We all laughed, but nobody relaxed. The tension came in and settled over us like a tangible presence. Suddenly it felt like there was a hidden motive behind every apparently casual move. Omar and I put our heads together, grinning and occasionally laughing as if we were telling jokes.

"You know them?" I whispered.

He laughed uproariously and said, "Oh, yeah!" out loud, then leaned forward and said, "We struck gold. The sideburns and moustache belong to Murales. That, as they say, is our man."

I laughed and said, "No, man!" so everyone could hear.

Omar laughed, too, and raised his voice to say, "Wait, man, there's more!" With our heads together again he said, "The one with the muscles is

Carlos Rivera. He works at the docks, but he's a munitions expert on the side...and we know which side."

More laughing. "Come on, Omar. You're not that old!"

"No! No!" he chuckled. "Wait! It gets better!" By keeping these inane remarks on a level with everyone else's chatter, we kept our neighbors from being curious about what they couldn't hear...we hoped. Anyway, his voice lowered again. "The skinny one is Hector Rodriguez, a sociology teacher who uses his classroom as a recruiting station. The black guy is Victor Jardine. He hates white folks. He thinks Marxism will help him drive whites off the islands."

"It didn't drive them out of Russia," I commented.

"Not funny."

Lorna came back with two full glasses while we were whooping it up over that. "Compliments of the Spanish Armada over there, gents!"

We picked up our glasses and turned around.

Well, we hadn't exactly tried to be totally invisible. It wouldn't have worked anyway; like trying to hide a giraffe in a barnyard.

I raised my glass high and addressed the newcomers. "To Queen Isabella!" I toasted.

Everybody thought that was hysterical, especially the Cubans. Jardine just glared. Well, according to what Omar had said, he wouldn't think very much or me or Queen Isabella.

"Hey, gringo!" Murales called to me. His friends thought that was funny, too. "You pretty funny. You always hang out with our black brothers?"

I shrugged. "I hang out with my friends, that's all. They come in all shapes, colors and sizes. When you like people, you get friends." I felt a pang when I realized I didn't really know what I was talking about.

That statement attracted Jardine's attention. "You like people?"

"Sure."

"All kinds?"

I shrugged again. "It all depends on the person."

He stood up. "I don't like all kinds," he said, drawing it out. "In fact, I don't like you."

Almost against my will, I found my body bracing itself. "Well!" I said, feigning offense, "I ain't buying you any drinks!"

That rated a laugh from the group, which was a good sign. He was one of them, and I was an outsider, but my friendliness in the face of his hostility was putting some of them on my side.

Jardine saw what was happening and something inside him snapped. He wasn't going to let it go any further. He flicked his wrist and a five-inch blade glinted in the dim light.

# *Chapter 17*

The knife itself didn't bother me. I'd faced uglier and more dangerous hardware and lived to laugh about it. What bothered me was the audience we had. If I lost this little scuffle, they'd all be mad at him, but that wouldn't help me much. The trouble was if I won, I wasn't sure they'd still be sympathetic to me.

Yeah, and what would I do with him when I won? Once upon a time that wouldn't even have been a question. Now I had a standard and a testimony to uphold, and Omar was watching.

I shook my head. "Sorry, mister," I said, "but I'm still not buyin' you any drinks."

There were a few laughs at that again, but not nearly enough to break the growing tension.

Someone in the shadows stood up. "Five bucks on Victor," he said.

Another one stood. "I think you're wrong, Willie. The white boy here ain't scared, not one little bit. I think he'll take him."

By the time all the bets were in, the room was evenly divided. Jardine didn't like that, but it was a relief to me. If that many were willing to put money on me to win, they wouldn't be angry at me if I did.

Jardine's confidence was shaken, but he tried not to let it show. "Well, come on! Make your move, man!"

I laughed. "You have the attitude, you have the blade, and you want me to come to you? Oh, no, Vickie. I'm not making this easy for you."

"Look at that," someone said. "He's turnin' chicken."

I wasn't sure who he was referring to until someone else said, "Chickie Vickie!" and started others laughing.

His face bloated with rage and he bellowed something I didn't understand as he lunged at me. Sidestepping was easy. It was the usual story: his anger was impairing his judgment and perceptions, and undermining the skill he was depending on, making things easier for me.

I grabbed his knife hand and twisted it in a direction it wasn't designed to go. There was a loud snap, the knife dropped and he screamed. Then I grabbed his other wrist and twisted his arm behind his back so he was doubled over. I looked up then and said, "Anybody got a car?"

Two hands went up. I pushed him away from me and said, "I'd appreciate it if one of you would take Vickie here to a doctor. I'll pay you back for any bills. I didn't want any trouble and I still don't."

Lorna spoke for the first time. "You ain't payin' for nothin'. He made the trouble. Let him pay for his own mendin'."

There was a chorus of grunts agreeing with her. Now that it was over, everyone was properly indignant.

Murales stood up, a smile on his face. He watched as Jardine was hustled out the door, then turned to me. "Bill, I would like to apologize for my friend."

I shrugged and grinned. "He's the only one who got hurt. Seems your friend should apologize...to himself."

"You handle yourself well," he went on. I could almost see the oil oozing out of him. He was trying to put me on the defensive again. "Where did you learn such impressive skills?"

I turned and picked up my glass, catching Omar's eye as I did so. He wasn't happy, but he gave me a quick nod to let me know he was ready for whatever might happen.

Turning back to my audience, I said, "I learned it on the street." I walked around the room, bringing all the people into the discussion. "I found out I hated manipulators. You know, guys who use other people and make them do things they're sorry about later. I hate bullies. I learned how to stick up for the little guys and send the dirtbags running. It felt good."

I caught different sets of eyes while I talked and caught approving nods and grins from several guys.

Now it was time for his punch line. "I wonder how someone who hates bullies and manipulators can stand to live in the United States? Your whole society is built on that kind of thing."

I grinned. "I admit we allow it to happen. It's the price of freedom. Why, once we even allowed Castro to con us into supporting him!"

He wasn't amused. In fact, I'd just pushed a dangerous button. It was obvious from the way his face changed; it hardened to choke back the snarl. But he wasn't really secure enough to make his move yet.

Omar spoke up. "Hey, Bill! Enough of this foolishness, man! We're gonna be late if we don't get movin'!"

I looked at my watch. "If you say so," I said, putting my glass down.

Lorna smiled. "I hope you two come back again. Don't let what happened upset you none."

I smiled back. "We won't," I promised. Then, just to be friendly, I waved to Murales. He nodded back, but his eyes weren't friendly.

# *Chapter 18*

Omar headed for the door and I followed. We kept a good pace walking back down the road.

"Just what are we going to be late for?" I asked.

"For a while I thought we gonna be the late Bill and Omar."

We heard the car engine starting behind us and looked at each other. "Time to slay another dragon, eh, Saint George?" Omar said, grinning.

"I'll be happy if we just stop the dragon from slaying us."

He shook his head. "Man, you really ain't the same."

The shoulders of the road were soft, so we each took one and kept walking. We'd done this before, but I'd been a different person then. Omar was thinking like that, too. He didn't want his survival to be depending on me if I was going to turn squeamish on him.

The car sounded like it was picking up speed. We had to time this carefully. If we waited too long, it would be going too fast and we'd be dead meat in the road. I caught his eye and nodded. We turned and ran back toward the car. The dark Chevy did what we wanted. They thought we'd try to run away so they could run us down, but now they were confused. The driver didn't know what to do. He touched the brakes, but not enough to stop. That was just what we needed.

I jumped and landed across the windshield. Even though I was braced for it, the remaining speed of the car knocked the wind out of me. I could feel Omar hit against the back windshield, then I reached in through the open driver's window. My fingers found a throat and squeezed while the brakes squealed.

A hand reached out from the passenger window and grabbed my foot as the car left the road and hit the sand. The bumping and lurching made him let go, but my hand didn't let go of that throat. After all, it was mine; I'd found it.

The wheels dug themselves into a hole and the car stalled. I let go of the throat and rolled, landing by the driver's side and crouching. The passenger door opened and I heard a scuffling, then a gunshot. It was time to do something. Keeping low, I moved to the rear of the car and peeked over.

Omar stood there with a .357 Magnum in his right hand.

I stood up and saw his adversary squirming in the sand as his eyes rolled over in death.

*That's the second death in two days on this case and you're not even trying, Donley. Nice going.*

I must have moaned or something. Omar spun on me. "Stow it, man! This is his piece, and he was getting' ready to blow me away with it! What did you want me to do, hey?"

Good question. What did I want him to do? He wasn't a Christian. Besides, his life had been on the line. But I remembered that little room in Bucharest, when I'd let an enemy "accidentally" kill herself instead of me. Carmen had turned those accusing eyes on me and said, "How can she get saved now?" I'd had no patience or time for it then. Now I understood. That's how I felt as I looked at the dead human shell with the big hole in it and watched the spreading red stain in the sand. How can he get saved now? I certainly hadn't given him much of a chance.

I turned away and opened the driver's door. He was still gasping, so I grabbed his shirt and dragged him out onto the sand.

"Well, here's one that'll talk to us," I said. Then I recognized the fear-crazed face and grinned. "Well, if it isn't our friend the taxi-driving, freelance, moonlighting photographer!"

"He don't look like he can talk to nobody," Omar remarked, coming around to join us.

He was faking the extent of his pain and we both knew it. I turned my back on his as he clutched his throat and groveled. He was really hurting, but he could talk to us if he wanted to.

"Well, if he can't tell us anything, you might as well waste him like the other one," I said.

"Wait!"

It was a hoarse croak. He made it sound worse than it really was, in the hope that we wouldn't know he was shamming.

Omar lifted him a bit and held him against the door. I pointed at him and said, "Murales sent you after us, didn't he?"

He started to nod, then his eyes got so wide they almost fell out. He screamed, and it seemed to go on long after he should have run out of breath. Then he started shaking and twitching. His teeth chattered and his eyes rolled back.

Omar let him go and he flopped to the ground but continued with the shakes. The scream became a moan, which in turn became a strange gurgling sound. And he never stopped for breath. Suddenly he arched his back and stayed like that, on his heels and shoulders. The rest of his body was rigidly in the air. After what seemed like a long time, his whole body relaxed and he slumped, his eyes and mouth wide open.

"Hey! He's dead!" Omar said, unnecessarily.

I started thinking out loud. "Maybe he had one of those hollowed out teeth, with the poison capsule in it. No, that doesn't really hold up. They wouldn't make it so painful."

Omar's eyes were big. He looked grimmer than ever, and when he spoke, it was slowly. "No, Bill. I seen this kinda thing before. He didn't dispatch himself. This guy was bein' controlled."

I looked at him. "Brainwashing?"

He shook his head.

"Implants under the scalp?"

He shook his head again, but this time he spoke; just one word.

"Voodoo."

# *Chapter 19*

We made sure there was nothing of interest in their pockets or in the car. Then we went back to Omar's place, and he made the clean-up call again ("Already? Twice in one day? Business boomin' for you, man! Ha! Ha!")

Omar went to his back porch and sat on a rocking chair, staring out at his lake....or Rosa's Lake. I gave him about fifteen minutes by himself before joining him. Then I just sat in a straight-back chair for another five minutes before I said, "How do you know it wasn't an implant?"

He rubbed his eyes and looked at me, with indignation at first, but the look changed to resignation. He seemed older, and very tired. "How do doctors know when it's chickenpox or when it's measles? 'Cause they know what they both look like. I know what voodoo looks like, and that was voodoo."

"Chickenpox and measles," I muttered. It didn't seem to me that childhood diseases had a whole lot to do with what we were talking about, but he could choose his own metaphors. It still left me in the dark, though. I didn't even know enough about this to ask the right questions. After a while we just settled down and took a rest.

Correction - he took a rest.

I stretched out on his couch, propped my head up and pulled out the pocket-sized Bible. There was something I'd read recently that I wanted to check out again. It didn't take long to find it. I was getting a little better at being able to find things...the parts I'd read already, anyway.

Two guys running out of a graveyard to Jesus. They were full of demons. "My name is Legion, for we are many". He commanded them to get out, but He let them take over a herd of pigs, which then killed themselves immediately.

Voodoo. People dying on command. Only a few days since I've become a Christian and I'm transported from a simple, materialistic "kill or be killed" existence into a world filled with spooks and hobgoblins. I'd always thought things became peaceful and joyous when someone became a Christian. Now it seemed that there was more conflict in my life than ever.

Then there was another place, where His disciples came and said, "Even the demons are subject to us in Your Name!"

And that brings the whole thing right into my backyard. Cuban Marxists and super weapons and voodoo and the kidnapping of an intelligence director. It's all up to Mrs. Donley's boy Billy to set things right.

A wild resentment started to rise up inside of me. I'd been forced into this assignment. It was supposed to have international significance. Well, okay. Here I am, trying to be a consistent Christian and a government counter-assassination agent, still pretty sure they both couldn't be done together.

"Jean Juares". The threat of war didn't seem to be here. Of course, the information locked in Chase's cranium would be an effective trigger in the wrong hands. Some of the stunts we'd pulled in the Middle East would spark a holy war if those Muslim fanatics ever heard about it. Add to that some of the scams and counter assassinations our little group has been responsible for in almost every country, including some of our allies, and the USA would become an international bull's-eye. They wouldn't care that most of our operations hadn't had official approval; that even the CIA wouldn't touch them. Yet with all that buildup, I find myself chasing Haitians in Vacationland.

"Heracles". In DC they'd called me that. I guess I should have been flattered, but it made me uncomfortable, probably because it was a pagan myth, though I didn't really know. Why couldn't they have found a Biblical name?

But that wasn't the main thing. Refusing this assignment would have been a capital crime, and that really burned me. After all the times I'd risked my life, gotten beat up, stabbed, shot (three times: once in the left arm, once in each leg), and all the insane situations I'd voluntarily put myself into, I could be executed for saying "no" just this once!

That was a selfish attitude, and I knew it. Would anyone else have found that note and gotten even this far? Probably, but she had written it to me.

Well anyway, this is the job and it's deadly and dangerous, hoorah. Three dead already, assuming Chase was still alive. All of them were on the opposition, and the opposition had killed most of them, unless the suicide in my apartment had been simply that. I'd been right there every time, but they'd killed their own men instead of me. If this kept up, they'd wipe themselves out before I had a chance to do much of anything.

Flippancy aside, the danger was real, and I knew it. So was the urgency. Even now Chase could be pumped full of the newest truth drug, singing her brains out to an eager audience.

Now things were getting dangerous in a different way. I'd come down here to find Chase. Going after Murales was only part of that; the only clue she'd given me. It was probably the only thing she had to give me.

But Murales wasn't leading me to Chase. He was sending me after illegal Haitians. And I wasn't after them. I've got nothing against Haitians; I don't care where they go to live. As far as I was concerned, they should be allowed to live wherever they wanted to. After all, I can go live anywhere I want to. Why shouldn't they be able to do the same thing?

It was beginning to look like I could be mixed up in two completely different matters. It was time to get back to basics. Finding Chase was my assignment. Anything else was a distraction, to be avoided. But that left me with yesterday's big question: How? Every lead I had brought me to a brick wall.

Trying to figure out what to do can be exhausting work. Somewhere in the middle of it I fell asleep.

The sleep was fitful, sweeping over me slowly and departing suddenly. My body wanted to sleep, but my mind refused to let go of the problem of Chase. How to get to her? Where and what was that super weapon? What should I do next?

Chase had wanted me to find Murales.

Chase was missing.

Murales was obviously interested in me.

And I wasn't trying to hide.

Suddenly I was sitting up in a dark room, sleep forgotten. They'd called me Heracles...the one who didn't want to fight in the Trojan War...the war that was supposedly won by a Trojan Horse...

I heard a stirring in the darkness and Omar said, "What's up, man?"

"Murales is going to come for me," I said.

There was a hesitation, then, "You sure?"

"Yeah, I'm real sure. It'll probably be tonight. I think we were being watched when we went to the Pirate's Cove, and he came in just to check me out. He's been waiting for me."

"So, how you wanna play it? We could take some hardware to the bushes to turn things around when they show up, or we can just put you in a hotel under some dingbat name. What you wanna do?"

"Nothing."

"Say what?"

"I'm going to let myself get taken. It's the quickest way to Chase, because he's got her; I'm sure of that. And, as much as I like your company, I want this assignment over. It's time to cut corners."

"Well...what you want me to do?"

"When they get here, we'll give a little resistance. Then you disappear and stay out of trouble, Octopus."

I heard the chuckle. "You guessed it, man. I'll call Kingpin. He'll send me on a little vacation 'till this blows over. What'll we do now?"

"We do what all the good little boys do," I said. "We go to bed and get some sleep."

# Chapter 20

"P sst! Bill!"

My eyes opened, blinked, and tried to focus. It was still night, and the room was dark. Omar was crouching three feet away from me, according to training. Never touch a sleeping agent; you don't know what his conditioned reaction will be. More than one knife or gun had done its work before the poor sleeper realized he was being asked how he liked his coffee.

"What's up?" I whispered back, without moving.

"Company outside, just like you said."

Now it was time to start moving. My feet hit the floor. "You see how many?"

Omar shrugged. "Don't know yet. Counted five so far."

I kept away from the window as I looked out. Two parked cars. Occasional movement behind them.

"Careless," I whispered.

"Why don't you forget this getting captured stuff and take 'em out? Piece of cake, if we do this right," Omar said, looking at me significantly.

I shook my head. "Blowing everyone away won't help me find Chase."

"Neither will gettin' blown away your own self."

"Then it won't be my problem anymore."

He sighed, ready to change the subject.

"Diversion?" I said.

He nodded. "Grenades."

"Good."

He went to get them and I kept watching. By the time he returned I'd counted five visitors. I hoped they were the same five he'd seen.

We each took one of the grenades and went to the back door. Standing silently to each side of the door so we wouldn't be seen from outside, we kept our eyes sweeping the area. Peripheral vision is better than direct vision in the dark, and finding movement is best of all. If nothing else is moving, then keep your eyes moving. They'll have a better chance of catching something that doesn't belong. I never understood the science behind that, but I knew it worked.

After watching for a while without noting any movement, we were ready for action.

"Looks like they're all out front," I whispered.

"Very careless," Omar said.

"But I don't for one minute believe that's all there are. I intend to be a little clumsy, but you want to stay free, remember?"

He gave me a look that was half-smirk and half-sneer. "Yes, papa." He opened the door. I slipped past him, outside, and to the left. Then he stepped out and moved to the right.

We pulled the pins out together and lobbed the grenades over the roof, but purposely wide of the mark. If any of those guys had wandered, there was nothing we could do for them now.

The explosions were almost simultaneous. The air rocked, my ears hurt, and Omar's windows blew out.

We ran.

I made for the line of bushes, braced for the gunshots over the roar of the grenades. As I reached them, I went into a somersault and covered my face.

The bushes did not welcome me. I wound up with bruises and scratches all over my body before rolling to a stop. I was on my back, braced to get into a crouch and run around to our visitors. Suddenly I was staring into the twin bores of a .12 gauge shotgun.

"Careless, Mr. Donley," Alfredo Murales said, grinning, "Very careless."

# Chapter 21

I relaxed. There was nothing I could do while that thing was pointed anywhere near me. Trust me: buckshot doesn't miss. Besides, this was what I had wanted to happen, right?

His smile faded, but his confidence didn't. He was waiting. It was my turn to say something. I was tempted to keep my mouth shut and wait him out, but that would probably have antagonized him, and I wasn't ready for that. I'd worry about throwing him off balance after finding Chase. After all, as I'd just recently reminded myself, that was the assignment.

"Hey," I said, "if you really want me to pay for Victor's treatment, just ask. I offered, remember?"

That wasn't what I was supposed to say. He gave me an "Oh, come off it!" kind of look and said, "Up."

Slowly, I got to my feet. I was the soul of cooperation. Then I dusted myself off with slightly exaggerated motions. Just like with Ninshka, I wanted him to get used to seeing me moving without getting alarmed or ready for a surprise.

Off to the right we heard two shots, followed by the panicked squawking of a few birds.

Murales grinned again. "Too bad about your friend. Keep that in mind if you start feeling rebellious."

I could have, and probably should have, kept my mouth shut then. Perhaps I should have gotten all emotional about my good buddy Omar, what I'd do to them, and so forth. That blustering threat of his had annoyed me too much. I didn't want to break all his bubbles just yet, but I felt the need to break at least one of them. "Oh, I figure I'm safe enough for now," I said.

He frowned. "Oh? Why is that?"

"At the Pirate Cove I was introduced as 'Bill'. No last name. Yet you know mine, as you so carelessly blurted out just now." My pointing out his own carelessness, after his smug use of the word at me, deepened his frown. "Well anyway, the main thing is that I'm still alive. If you just wanted to get rid of me, there would be pieces of me all over this yard. You want something from me."

I should have said something else. It might have kept the conversation going. As it was, he said, "Very clever. But not very impressive. Let's go around to the front, shall we?"

We marched around to the front of the house. Needless to say, I was in the lead. It was gratifying to see that all the car windows had been shattered by the grenades' blast. Murales' project was getting expensive. This kind of surprise always gave subordinates something to have second thoughts about...especially if they'd used their own cars.

I slowed my pace when I reached the cars and ignored the hostile glares of the four men who stood behind them. Trying to look inconspicuous riding in those was going to be amusing.

Behind me, Murales said, "Where's Tyrone?"

They shrugged or shook their heads in silence.

I grinned. "Too bad about your friend."

That rattled him. I was talking too much these days. He pushed the shotgun against my spine and snarled, "Move on!"

We continued walking in silence. About fifteen minutes later we came to another car--this one a Cadillac--and I was ushered into the back seat on the passenger's side. One young black man was already sitting behind the driver's seat, which was also occupied, and another followed me in. I was neatly wedged in the middle. Murales got into the front and we drove off.

I settled back comfortably to enjoy the ride. I tried inane conversation, but they all ignored me. There were things I could have done to make them acknowledge me, but I decided it wouldn't be worth it. I needed information, and I hoped I was on my way to it.

We continued through the sleeping town to the docks. Nobody spoke, which at this point was fine with me.

Lord, I need You now. I could get myself out of this easily, but that wouldn't help Chase. Besides, You wouldn't appreciate it. The lives of my enemies are suddenly important to me, and mine isn't to them. I'm probably putting my head into a hungry lion's mouth, because I don't know what else to do. I'm not even certain I'm getting closer to Chase. Even that's more of a hope than anything else. I really need You now, Lord.

There was a casino on the dock that was still going strong, so I could hope nothing drastic was going to happen right there.

Cocking my head toward the casino, I quipped, "Well, if you guys wanted a fifth hand for Old Maid, you just had to ask."

Nobody laughed. Nobody even smiled. If the baggage wants to say dumb things, we'll just ignore it and maybe it'll shut up and behave. The driver pulled right out onto the pier and stopped between yachts. It looked like an empty space until I saw somebody's head raise up and realized there was a motorboat moored there.

Murales said, "Here we are."

I felt a stinging in my left shoulder and looked. The guard was holding an empty syringe, and grinning at me. "Nighty-night, man."

I slept.

# *Chapter 22*

I was vaguely aware of being loaded onto a boat and traveling for hours. Someone got seasick; it might have been me. Finally, hands lifted me off the boat and I was put on a stretcher. We bounced along endlessly until I was dumped on the ground, aware of the unevenness and discomfort.

Slowly, slowly, control of my senses came back to me, along with a massive headache. When I was able to sit up, I did so and looked around. I was in a corrugated shack with one door and one window. I sat up, watching the dust particles in the light, and sweating.

Shaking my head, I got slowly to my feet and stumbled to the window. At first I was blinded. I had to keep blinking until I could see. My sense of direction was shot, but I figured it was late in the day. There's a kind of change in the sunlight as the day goes on. It seems white in the morning and yellowish in the afternoon.

The shack was in a clearing, which seemed surrounded by jungle. There were several other shacks, apparently in a circle, and a dance floor sized space in the middle of it all.

There was a lot of activity. Dark, glistening bodies bustled in every direction, with an apparent sense of urgency. As I stood and watched, trying to make sense of the action, I found I was right: the sun was going down.

There was a table about seven feet long and four feet wide in the center of the clearing. Several tall poles surrounded it, and then there was a large space. Finally, right outside the shacks, was a circle of benches, three deep.

There were footsteps outside the door, at least two people, and someone started to fumble with the door. I had two choices. I could stand there and show them I was big and strong and unafraid, or I could get back down on the ground and pretend I was still unconscious, in the hope that they'd speak more freely and I'd learn something.

Some choice.

I hit the deck just before the door opened. One set of footsteps entered and the door closed. Forcing myself not to brace against a possible kick, I kept my breathing as shallow as I could.

"There is no way you could still be unconscious, so let's cut all the dirtbag tricks, Donley."

It was Murales, of course. I decided stubbornness wouldn't help at this point, so I opened my eyes and sat up.

He was unarmed, but standing across the shack, against the opposite wall. "Before you try anything," he said, "there are five AK-47s trained on the door, just in case the wrong man steps out."

I grinned. "Thanks. That's quite a compliment. Unless you just believe in overkill."

He shrugged. "I like that number. It reminds me of the Pentagram. But I didn't come in here just to brag about my firepower."

I put on one of my more skeptical looks. "But you did come in here to brag about something."

He nodded. "Yes. It's important to me that you know certain things. You think you've been winning fights and learning clues and making progress. That's not true. I've been in control since the beginning. Your boss did what I wanted her to do, and you did what I wanted you to do."

So I am getting closer to Chase after all. That gave me a boost. "Thank You for that much, Lord," I thought.

Murales went on. "The one who died at your home in Washington, DC, and the one who died on Great Inagua yesterday did so at my command. What do you think of that?"

I was hoping he wouldn't ask. "No comment."

He nodded again. "The expected reaction. You think I'm crazy. I can see this. That's okay. Before you die, you will be a believer."

His use of the word "believer" struck a chord. "Oh, that's right," I said. "You're the religious communist."

"Communist?" Contempt was in his eyes as well as his voice. "Communism will never work; it's too plastic and one-dimensional. No form of materialism has any lasting answers."

I agreed with that much, but I felt he was going where I wouldn't want to follow. "Answers to what?" I blurted.

He didn't hesitate. "Power. That's really the bottom line in this world. Power over nature, power over people. Just power."

"Power as a means to what?"

Murales shook his head. "You do not understand. Power is it, man. It's not a means to anything. It's the goal. Everything we say and do is a means of gaining power over somebody or something."

The speech was winding down. I wanted to keep him talking, so I prodded him. "Every communist regime I've ever seen was into just that: getting and keeping power over people."

"Oh, they are, they are." He was relaxing now, warming to his theme. "But they'll never really get it. They're materialists. They don't understand or accept spiritual things. Now that's where real power is: in the supernatural. As long as communism rejects the supernatural, they will remain pawns for those of us who really understand power."

While he was talking, I remembered Omar and what he'd said. "So where is this power then? Voodoo?"

His eyebrows went up. "That's part of it. It's the 'old religion'. We call it 'wicca'."

I didn't think I'd heard it right. I repeated what it sounded like. "You mean witchcraft?"

He shook his head impatiently. "No, no. That's just what the Church called it to give it a bad name. It's really like...like an empathy with the elemental forces of nature. Once you can control them, people are a piece of cake, man."

"I've seen wicca types on news programs and such. They always claim they're good guys; they have a benevolent religion."

"Yes, and they believe it, too. And, while they're busy making herbal headache remedies and being high profile, I'll be free to stay underground and accomplish what really matters."

Now it was time to goad him with a little sarcasm. "And all this power is being used against an obscure little cloak-and-dagger group that almost nobody even knows about. That's very impressive."

"Is that what you think?" He was genuinely amused. Now that he was in total control of the situation, he was downright friendly. "You spoke of power as a means to an end. I corrected that. Now I'll correct the rest of it. Your little group is the means. You're not even the real target."

"Oh? Then who is?"

His smile broadened. "Come on, man. One guess."

"Okay, it's the president. What's going to happen to him?"

"He is going to die tonight."

"You're gonna kill him?"

He stepped to the door. "Not in any way you could prove in court. He'll just fall down and die, right in front of whoever is with him."

"Sounds like a tall order."

"It is, it is. There are lots of Christians praying for his welfare. Overcoming that needs a special offering."

"A special offering?" I said, as in, "Wha...?"

Just before stepping through the door, he told me, "The blood of an unwilling sacrifice."

# Chapter 23

Throughout the rest of the afternoon I sat and cooked under the metal roof of my prison. Several times I tried to get some sleep, knowing it was necessary. My fatigue was my enemy's weapon. I knew that from experience. Drug-induced sleep is never as good as the real thing. But it was too hot for sleep, so I just lay there on my back or sat cross-legged, doing as little as possible, conserving my energy in the hope that I would need it.

As the sun went down, the shack cooled off quickly. It never really got cold, but the sudden change started me shivering.

The thoughts came, a series of jumbled memories that drew their own conclusions and pulled me into them.

"I've been in control since the beginning."

"...it's true, Olga; He does take care of us."

"Your boss did what I wanted her to do, and you did what I wanted you to do."

"I don't pretend to understand why this happened, but I'm trusting You to work it out for Your glory."

"This guy's bein' controlled...Voodoo."

"Power. That's really the bottom line in this world. Power over nature, power over people. Just power."

"Even as the Son of Man came not to be ministered unto, but to minister, and to give His life a ransom for many."

Some other passages came back to me from the Bible I'd been reading. They were things Jesus had said to His disciples.

"Behold, I give unto you power to tread on serpents and scorpions, and over all the power of the enemy; and nothing shall be any means hurt you."

"But ye shall receive power, after that the Holy Ghost is come upon you: and ye shall be witnesses unto Me..."

So Murales was wrong; wrong where he thought he had some secret, special knowledge about power. Wrong, wrong. Real power is a means to an end; power as an end is a lie; an enslavement.

Real power...

Carmen and border guards. That was real power.

It was time to stop thinking, stop trying to sleep, and start praying.

The drums started first. A primitive, hypnotically repetitious rhythm that seemed to be trying to pull me into itself. I went to the window to check out the situation. This time the activity was less urgent. It had a ritualistic, almost automated, quality about it. Omar's words, "Bein' controlled" came back to me again, and I could see it now.

Torches were lit and tied to the poles, until the entire clearing flickered crazily in the uncertain light. More people started to arrive, dressed in colorful native costumes, swaying and jerking to the drumbeat. Some of them brought their own folding chairs, but most left their things on a bench and joined the dance. They seemed to be ignoring each other once they started with the moves. I was reminded of millions of American kids with their boom-boxes, but I couldn't think about that theme long enough to come to any conclusions about it.

Soon a chant began, in a language I didn't understand. Even the voices seemed to be subservient to the beat. The drum was like a pied piper, leading the people into a sensual, rhythmic mindlessness.

Something was wheeled into the clearing on two dollies. As three men clumsied it into an upright position, the drumming became a little more insistent and frantic. The people responded, their dancing and swaying movements becoming more violent and whip-like. The chanting occasionally took on a wailing quality that rose and fell in waves.

Then I saw what the thing was: a life-sized human figure, crudely fashioned out of papier-mache. It was dressed in a conservative suit, and where the face should have been was plastered a picture of the President of the United States.

A hush fell over the group and someone stepped out of the shack across from mine. He wore a loincloth, a crown of twigs, a necklace of bones, and carried a kind of scepter with a skull on the end of it. His face was painted with white, black and red streaks, but I recognized him.

It was Alfredo Murales, the "Marxist" whose "religion" was frowned on by his employers. For once, I agreed with the communists. I was frowning on his brand of religion, myself.

He signaled to someone I couldn't see and the drumming started again, much slower this time. Murales went to the big table-thing and selected two long-bladed knives. Several other men did the same thing, though still enslaved to the drumbeat.

An awed murmur went up from the crowd. Then two men were dragging out the first sacrifice, feeble but struggling.

Unconsciously, I whistled, though I wasn't really surprised.

I'd found Chase.

# *Chapter 24*

She was tired, way past the point of exhaustion. The fight left in her was a hybrid combination of will power and desperation. After they had tied her to the table, which was apparently an altar, they came over to my shack. That suited me fine. I wanted to be where the action was. I still wasn't sure what I'd do when I got there, but at least I'd have options.

The door opened and one of them stepped in. He stood next to the door and stared at me, waiting. At this point, I was willing to oblige. I stepped out the door and into the arms of my adoring public. They all stared at me with cold-fish eyes as I made my way through the benches, my royal escort within arm's reach.

Chase recognized me immediately, but had the presence of mind to keep that fact to herself.

When we entered the circle in the middle of the clearing, my guards each grabbed an arm and twisted it behind my back. I was expecting it and relaxed. It didn't hurt as much as it was supposed to.

Murales was smiling at me. "How do you like my little Haitian village, Mr. Donley?"

Now the connection with Haiti was clear, and his bi-weekly disappearances from the Bahamas.

"We're in Haiti?" I asked, brilliantly.

He didn't seem to think that rated an answer. He shook his scepter at me and paced back and forth, babbling something the Haitians appreciated. Then the ceremony continued.

A strange lethargy came over me. I thought I heard Chase calling me, but the chanting and the flickering light just made me so sleepy...

The drums began to fill up my attention, becoming more attractive and more demanding. The colorful figures weaving and bobbing to the beat began to lose their focus, becoming vague blurs in the torchlight. A few older women in the front row sat down. Everyone else kept swaying and stepping.

Then the darkness around the camp seemed to close in, shrinking the circle of light and color I was in. And that was proper. The whole idea was for the lights and colors to be swallowed up by the darkness...

A little, nagging voice in the back of my mind said, "You'd better do something, Bill."

In my mind I answered, "Uh...yeah, I guess I'd better," but all I really wanted to do was sleep...

Then a memory flashed in my mind. I was a toddler, on my mother's lap, and she was singing. She was teaching me a song...

That's it, I thought. Sing the song. That's the thing to do. The thing is to sing. The song is the thing. Sing the thing. Sing the song. If I can't help myself, at least I can give them a hard time about doing me in.

I shook myself and started bellowing the song my mother had taught me: "JESUS LOVES ME, THIS I KNOW..."

The effect was more than I'd bargained for. The chanting stopped, lights and colors came back into focus, and a collective gasp went up.

"FOR THE BIBLE TELLS ME SO!"

Murales rolled his eyes, arched his back, opened his mouth wide...and howled. His voice seemed to come from the bottom of a deep well. It was the wail of a hopelessly trapped beast. It rose to a crescendo before he bit it off and glared at me with so much hatred I could feel it.

Meanwhile the two goons reacted in different ways. The one on my right relaxed his grip, and the one on my left tightened his. I yanked my right arm where his thumbs were and it was free. Then I put all my weight into the fist that rammed his chin and he went down.

My left foot went up and I rammed it downward, gritting my teeth and squeezing my eyes in the effort. I felt the bones crunch as that one's foot gave way under mine and my left arm was free also.

Without thinking, I grabbed the torch pole behind me and pulled it out of the ground. While I was doing that, I remembered what I'd read, when Paul cast a demon out of somebody...

"I command thee in the name of Jesus Christ..."

Of course, he'd only had one person to deal with at the time, and I now had something like a hundred. But then, the principle ought to work anyway, regardless of numbers.

I swung the long pole, yelling, "In the Name of Jesus Christ..." and realized I didn't know what to tell them to do. Finally I just said, "Scatter! Get outta here in Jesus' Name!" and let the pole, torch and all, fall into the seats. The wood of the benches made good kindling, and it didn't take long for a respectable blaze to spring up.

Pandemonium took over. It looked like the people were turning on each other, grabbing throats, babbling and tearing hair. I was on my way to another torch when I saw Murales. He'd decided to go through with the ceremony, interruptions notwithstanding, and was getting ready to plunge a long, carved knife into Chase's midsection.

She was looking at me, her face twisted with desperation, and yelling. I couldn't hear her with all the noise, but I knew it was time to leave the crowd alone and get back to specifics.

I dropped the pole I had and started running back to the altar. I didn't think I'd moved very far away from it, but it seemed way too far now. Chase was wriggling frantically, uselessly, against the ropes. I yelled, "Hey, stop!" at Murales, but he chose not to hear me.

The blade went up and hovered. Murales' eyes bulged and his face became flushed and bloated in anticipation of his triumph.

There wasn't time. Oh, dear Lord, he was going to do it and there wasn't enough time for me to get there and stop him.

Unless...

I pointed at him and shouted, "Don't you DARE, in Jesus' Name!" I don't think he really heard me, but his head jerked up and his arm stopped in mid-stroke. I caught his eye and held it. He was frozen, his face a mask of hate, lips quivering. He looked like he was trying to talk, but all that came out was a long, wavering moan. A few flecks of foam appeared at the corners of his mouth, his eyes rolled back into his head, and he keeled over backwards.

I ran to the altar, stooping to pick up the knife Murales had dropped when he fell, and sawed the knots that held Chase down. They cut easily. She sat up quickly and looked around at the madness.

"Some super weapon, huh?" I commented.

She swallowed, her eyes even bigger than usual, confusion and bewilderment giving her a wandering, dazed look. "You...you did this?"

I shook my head. "Not exactly. Let's get out of here."

Her legs were numb from the ropes, and I had to carry her at first.

The crowd wasn't even trying to get away anymore, much less stop us from leaving. They had even turned on themselves. One woman was holding her hand in the flames of a burning bench, just sitting there, screaming.

Several others were gashing themselves with knives. Two women were trying to pull a man's dreadlocks out, and he seemed content to let them.

Meanwhile, the growing, spreading flames hurled writhing shadows across the ground.

After that I stopped looking. So much for that religion. If this was the "elemental force...of nature", that they have "empathy with", they could keep it.

On the outskirts of the madness, I put Chase down carefully, making sure she could hold herself up. When her feet were on the ground and she was standing on her own, she stared at all the insane horror and muttered, "All you did was sing that song..."

"No time for that now," I said. "Do you know how to get to the dock?"

She nodded and pointed. "You're right. Let's get out of here!"

With Chase right behind me, I pushed and kicked my way through the last part of the crazed mob. Then we quietly slipped between shacks into the jungle.

The night animals had been shocked into silence by the human spectacle. Aside from that, the dark foliage seemed strangely warm and welcoming as we pushed our way carefully through the weeds.

# *Part 3:*

## LAMBS, WOLVES AND LIONS

# *Chapter 1*

We made it to the dock, exhausted, and crouched in bushes while we caught our breath. I couldn't see anything at the dock except a good-sized yacht was anchored a few hundred feet out.

When Chase had enough breath, she gasped, "Rowboat."

*Aha,* I thought. *She means there's a rowboat tied to the dock, even though I can't see it. Brilliant, Donley. You're on a roll.*

"We go to the yacht, right?"

She just nodded.

That was when I heard the noise behind us. Murales' congregation was looking for us. And it wasn't to express their gratitude.

The rowboat...and whatever was waiting for us on the yacht...suddenly looked better. I stood up, surprised at how cramped and stiff my muscles were.

Chase stood, too, and groaned a little.

Without speaking, we limpingly hurried down the dock until we saw the rope tied around a mooring post to our left.

Jumping into the boat was nightmarish. Both of us sure we'd overcompensate for our cramped muscles and wind up in the water, or capsize the little boat, that we took too long about it. Then, getting our sea legs seemed to take an hour or so, while I fumbled with the knot.

By the time I had the boat untied and was pulling at the oars, they were swarming all over the dock. They weren't exactly shouting or screaming, but I was glad I couldn't understand what I could hear.

I was concerned when I saw a few of them actually jump in and swim after us. Fortunately, their strokes couldn't match my oars.

After what felt like forever, I pulled the oars in and reached for the bottom steps of the stairway...excuse me, ladder.

We tried to be silent, but as I got to the top, I knew we'd failed at that. A hand grabbed my wrist as I looked back to check on Chase. I'd figured that, in this case, the gentlemanly thing to do was to go first and check for danger.

I tensed, ready to do the twist-grab-and-pull routine, when a familiar voice said, "It's okay, Bill. It's only me."

"Omar?" I came up the rest of the way and stumbled onto the deck.

Explanations would have to wait. Chase was right behind me, limp and rubbery.

Omar let me have her weight. "I'll lead the way. Let's get her to a bunk. Then we can talk."

I caught his eye and he knew the unasked - talk about what? He just turned and led the way.

We got Chase bedded down, in spite of some feeble protests on her part, and were soon seated in the kitchen...excuse me, galley.

Omar was pouring drinks. "I know you don't partake of the hard stuff anymore, but this is plain red wine. You'll be needing it."

"That sounds encouraging." I took the glass without taking my eyes off him. "What happened to your accent?"

"That's why I'm here. It seems that my cover has been seriously compromised on Great Inagua, so I'm being recalled from Paradise."

"Oh. I'm sorry."

"Ah, don't be. I've been on borrowed time for years."

"It seems to have had a real heavy effect on your speech patterns."

"Well, I was agent-in-place, so I had to act like I belonged there."

I almost asked, "Even to fellow agents?" But I knew the answer to that one: especially to fellow agents. There was no percentage in giving away information that might cost your life, even to a friendly.

"Besides, I'm not really sorry to leave. Though I'm sure you won't agree, my new assignment sounds like fun."

"Really? Can you share about it?"

"I not only can; I've been instructed to tell you."

I was having a hard time following this "new" Omar, without the accent and jive talk. That's why it took me a moment to catch his implication.

"Don't tell me it's another assignment!"

"Not for you. I'm the one who's been drafted this time. But I don't think you're going to want to miss this one."

I wanted to make some kind of "that's what you think" remark, but his face was too serious, almost resentful. I kept my mouth shut.

He picked up an unlabeled videotape. "This was delivered to me yesterday, not too long after you were taken. While you were busy rescuing the damsel and saving the world, I went over this little item a thousand times, trying to build a strategic response."

I'd never exactly thought of Chase as a "damsel", but I decided not to challenge the point.

Without another word, he pushed the tape into the VCR and hit the remote. The picture that came on shook the fatigue out of my system and left me shaking with an adrenaline rush that almost made me pass out.

There was Vladimir Ninshka, or whatever name he was using now, leering back at me.

"I must confess," Ninshka began, "that I do not know the exact agency for which William Donley works. Therefore, I am sending this to CIA headquarters in Langley, Virginia. I have confidence that this will reach him very shortly."

It was the same hypocritical urbane manner that he'd used on me in Bulgaria, but there was something else about him this time; something I couldn't quite put my finger on...

"I have had to leave Eastern Europe in rather a hurry, I'm afraid. A decision was made regarding me of which I became aware. My latest employers understood I was not a dedicated communist, but they respected my abilities. However, when Mr. Donley so generously left me alive, nobody over there believed I was honestly working for them. It seems the notorious Donley would never leave a true enemy alive. The bump on the head could well have been something agreed upon. Therefore, we must have been in league. I am now a target of the Eastern Bloc. I am called a traitor and slated for death.

"Donley's last word to me included the injunction to 'get saved'. Strange words from one whose reputation is murderous. I assume something happened to him to make him thus. 'Get saved,' he told me. This I plan to do. Not with your God, of course, but with my former employers, who are now my hunters. I will 'save' myself from them, and Donley, he will help me to do this."

I remembered. I hadn't been talking to him, and I was sure he'd been unconscious. But, somehow, he remembered those two words.

"I have one chance, I believe, to redeem myself. Those are two words Donley should appreciate now: 'believe' and 'redeem'. He should appreciate my position all the more. My 'redemption', if you please, will be accomplished by terminating Donley and returning the charming Ms. Gonsalo to Romania. Once Donley is dead, I can bring Ms. Gonsalo back to the country she belongs in.

"Therefore, I have come to the United States; to the land of freedom and democracy; to 'the land of the free, and the home of the brave', to confront William Donley.

"It has occurred to me that Donley may not wish to be confronted. Perhaps he has already retired from this dirty and deadly world. I have prepared for this possibility. Notice - " He stepped to his right and there she was, tied to a chair, dark head lolling on her shoulders. "Here," he went on, "is Ms. Gonsalo. I have every intention of presenting her to my former employers, and I am able do it. First, I wish to give Mr. Donley an opportunity to rescue her once again, this time on his native soil.

"I will be leaving, with Ms. Gonsalo, in one week. I am trusting that Donley will find me and will pacifistically die.

"The key, the stone you must move, if you will, is this: I am in a place where this Bible Donley has embraced is revered. Come to me preaching, shouting of judgment and hellfire, and I will find you. I will confront, not ambush...because I believe I shall win against you this time.

"Come to me, William Donley! We have much to resolve between us!"

With that, the screen went blank.

But I kept seeing Carmen, drugged or unconscious, slouched in that chair. Carmen, Carmen, why does it suddenly hurt so much to see you like that? I treated you so badly, and left you so suddenly, and now I'm the one who suddenly feels incomplete and bereft, just seeing you like that.

Anger and fear and fatigue started to war inside me and left me shaking, staring, and knowing there was one more thing I had to do before my life's direction could change.

Carmen!

"Bill? You okay?"

I wasn't, but I nodded anyway. "Have you got any thoughts on where they are? I mean, compared to his usual stomping grounds, every place in America 'reveres' the Bible."

"Well, I've been thinking about the infamous Bible Belt."

"That's in the South, right?"

"Yeah. From...oh, Virginia, I'd say, through Texas to Oklahoma. Some people include the Dakotas, but I think they're more into hippies and New Age stuff these days. The thing is, that's a large territory."

Then Chase's voice came from the doorway. "No, no, no. That's not where they are."

Omar looked up and past me. I turned. Exhausted and bedraggled, but on her feet, was Chase. She was leaning against the wall...excuse me, bulkhead...and shaking her head with a tired disgust.

I wasn't in the mood for games. "Yeah, so where are they?"

"He told you, Bill. Weren't you listening? Omar, rewind it a little and play it back."

He did so, and we heard Vlad go on until he said, "The key; the stone you must move..." and she said, "Okay, stop." When the screen was dark again, she said, "Well, didn't you hear it?"

Omar and I looked at each other, then back at her. He finally said, "Okay, I know I'm going to feel stupid for asking, but hear what?"

Chase rolled her eyes. "'The key...the stone'. A place that reveres the Bible. He's in the 'Keystone State': Pennsylvania. That's where the Amish, the Mennonites and the Moravians are. There are probably more churches in that state than in the entire Bible Belt."

"Well, that narrows it down a bit."

"But we're still talking about quite a few million people. It's a smaller haystack, but it's still a haystack."

"Maybe not," I said.

Omar looked at me, knowing there was more.

"Well, he's doing to me what I did to Murales. He acts like he's hiding, but he's not. He wants me to find him. He doesn't really want to leave the States without leaving one very dead Bill Donley behind him. So there's got to be a way to zero in on where he is."

Chase entered the conversation again. "You can eliminate the big cities then, for several reasons. He could hide easily in them and they don't revere the Bible like rural areas. So that lets out Philly, Pittsburgh and Scranton."

"That still sounds like a lot of hilly woods to comb through."

"It is. Like Bill said, Ninshka wants to be found. I'm sure he's already planted signposts to follow."

Omar took a sip of his wine. "The only thing we really need to figure out is the starting point."

"That's the going theory, anyway," I muttered.

"And," Chase concluded, "that's all the intelligence I can offer. I'm going to sleep for about a week, if you two don't mind."

Omar grinned. "The orders were to fly out of Great Inagua. Are you saying we should sail to the Florida Keys?"

"You just follow your orders."

# Chapter 2

Omar ordered me to bed soon after that. I found a bunk, sure I wouldn't sleep at all, I couldn't, I was too churned up, I...

Suddenly hot sunlight was bothering my eyes. "Let's go, Saint William," Omar said, nudging me. "You can make the coffee, since I'm the one who's officially working. Man, I thought you'd be up before dawn to do your devotions."

"Do my what?" I slurred, swinging my feet to the cold deck.

He stared at me, then shook his head and grinned. "You really are new to this, aren't you? Oh, well. Get in the shower and make with the coffee, man. I need you to help me with my homework before we dock."

"Homework?" I really wanted to know what he was talking about. But he ignored me and went upstairs...excuse me, topside.

I found the shower and took care of myself, leaving dripping underwear draped over the stall. After that it was easy. The coffee maker was a simple affair and Omar and I soon had steaming mugs in our hands.

"Chase still down?"

He nodded. "Yeah, that's okay. She's not used to fieldwork. Maybe after this we'll all get raises, huh?" Then he realized who he was talking to and added, "That is, if you stay."

I shrugged. "I'll probably leave, though I don't know. I think she wants me to stay, even though I sure messed up the Romanian assignment."

"Yeah, that's the kind of thing I was afraid you'd do to me down here. Seems that somehow you did the opposite. You managed to rough things up so badly that everybody knew the one who did it was the one who stayed with me the last day or so. But hey, these assignments rarely work out exactly the way they're supposed to. You know that."

"Yeah, but it never bothered me like this before."

"That's because you never let yourself get sweet on some young lady before."

A defensive hostility rose up inside of me and I came very close to telling him some things. He saw it and grinned at me.

I let it go, reluctantly, and shrugged. "So, you don't think I'll hinder you this time?"

"I won't let you. Last time it was your assignment. I was helping you, and I felt like all the responsibility was with me, but none of the clearance or authority. This time it's mine. You're along for the ride...and bargaining power. My job is to get that turkey out of the country...or make him disappear...without the girl. I hope to dangle you like fish bait. What I do with him then is none of your business."

Chase's voice surprised me. "But if he's not along in an official capacity," she said, "that makes him a private citizen. As such, he pays your salary. He's your boss by default."

Omar glared at her. "Hey, whose side are you on?"

She glared right back. "I thought we were all on the same side. Besides, you're forgetting who just saved my life." She grabbed a mug and the coffeepot and poured herself a full cup, black. "I'm still trying to figure out what I'm going to put in my report."

"Yeah," I said. "It had better be a masterpiece."

"What do you mean?"

"The Secretary of Defense wasn't sure you'd come back voluntarily. He gave me appropriate instructions if you didn't."

"Dispatch?"

I nodded.

She became thoughtful.

Omar glared some more. "Man, I'm in sterling company here. One gets religion and can hardly function, and the other goes AWOL just to stir up a bee's nest. No wonder they're calling me home!"

"You're breaking my heart, Omar," Chase muttered. "Besides, I'm hardly a fugitive, and you'll be rid of me as soon as we get to Miami."

"Planning to be a prodigal daughter, are you?"

"I thought Donley was the Bible freak."

Since I was being treated like a piece of furniture, I got off the stool and stepped outside, taking a deep breath. Even though I couldn't make out the words anymore, I could still hear their continued bickering. Trying to change channels in my brain, I let the soft rolling of the deck, the salty smell and the endlessness of ocean have all my attention.

Well, "endlessness" is too strong a word, I admit. A large island was off to my right, and fishing boats were here and there, beyond hailing distance. There was still a lot of water, and it helped me relax and think.

Bait, he'd called me. From a top agent with a security clearance, now I was the expendable worm squirming on the end of a hook.

Strangely, that didn't bother me. In fact, it helped me begin to form a strategy of my own. Omar wouldn't be as careless with Carmen's life as he was planning to be with mine, but it wasn't his primary purpose here. Suddenly, it was mine.

This wasn't something I was looking for. I hadn't fallen for anybody since Basha, the girl in Poland who'd claimed to be a Catholic underground worker but was actually being paid by the Party. She'd tried to kill me one night. The resultant struggle was brief and clumsy, but I left a piece of myself with that body and never missed it...until now, that is.

Now, of all people, Carmen Gonsalo! I mean, we hadn't even gotten along! We'd barely said a civil word to each other. But somehow, when I wasn't looking, I'd fallen for the dark-eyed Cuban Christian radical.

And I hadn't been looking. I'd been perfectly content with the one-night stands and the casual affairs to get the hormonal monkey off my back. Of course, that kind of thing was no longer an option. I hoped I wasn't playing games with my own head because of that.

The bickering downstairs...excuse me, below...was continuing. Those two were becoming a match made in heaven. Under the circumstances, that was a sour thought. I found a deck chair and snoozed.

# Chapter 3

The plane trip that took us from Great Inagua was a bumpy but silent ride, with everyone lost in his or her own thoughts. I nibbled on peanuts and drank cola...which was about all they offered.

Chase pulled me aside before we headed for different gates at the Miami International Airport. She seemed nervous and fidgety. "I know I won't see you again," she said. "You're welcome back...with whatever stipulations you want to make...if you decide to come. I think I understand a little better now. If you don't return, I do wish you all the best."

There was a whole lot I could have said then: smart remarks, profound challenges, and sentimental slush. All I could do was nod.

She seemed to understand. Stretching up on her toes, she kissed me on the cheek before turning and striding off to her nonstop flight to Dulles.

She didn't look back, or even break stride.

Omar was standing by our gate. His suitcase was different; it had changed in the few minutes we'd been apart. It was bigger and looked heavier. He was also holding a briefcase he didn't have before. Obviously, he'd found time for a briefing while I was saying goodbye to Chase.

When he saw me, he chuckled. "Wipe your cheek, Galahad. If Miss Gonsalo sees that, she won't understand."

I sneered at him and wiped my cheek with a tissue. "Hey, at least you're still employed."

He shrugged. "Maybe not, after these last few days. And especially after my last conversation with Chase."

"Not to worry. I usually made her angrier with my sarcastic remarks about the importance of the jobs we were given."

"Yeah, but I never saved her life."

"Neither did I, until the other day. Besides, she's not the one who's been briefing you lately."

He left that last item alone. They called our flight and we picked up our luggage, got in line and found our way through the accordion to our seats. After we found our seats and settled in, I pulled out my little pocket Bible and set it on the tray in front of me, ready to throw my nose into it if the company got tiresome, which I had a suspicion it would before long.

Omar had a surprise for me. He opened his briefcase and took out a Walkman, a set of cassettes, and a huge leather bound Bible. When he caught me staring, he waved at my little one and said, "You just go on with your devotions there, son. I've got homework to do."

"Homework? That's... Oh, no! You're not going as a preacher!"

"That's right. A Holy Ghost, Bible-thumpin' devil-stompin' Jesus lovin' man of some cloth or other."

"But...but you?"

"Yes, me! They couldn't pick you, Bill. Come on, face it! You're too sincere! You'd never agree to do this just to trap the bad guy. It all means too much to you. So, I'm on assignment, and you're my un-sanctioned shadow. As long as you behave yourself, that is."

"As long as I..." I stopped trying to argue. There really wasn't any point. He was right, and he was being nicer than he had to be about it.

"Actually, I'm kind of glad you're along," he said, expansively. "I may need some help finding certain passages, or explaining this Christian stuff. You'll be right there to bail me out."

"You're a funny guy. I've been saved less than a month, and you think I'm a seminary professor."

"Shoot, you're a lot closer to one than I've ever been. For instance, what verse got you saved?"

"What verse?" I was totally confused by that. "Well, no one verse. I just...I sort of...well...Carmen did show me some verses about being ransomed. I guess they did it, somehow."

"Yeah, but what were they? Where are they?"

"Uh...the New Testament?"

He shook his head. "You'll have to do better than that. You will be called upon to testify, so you better have that stuff ready, okay?"

I didn't answer. I couldn't.

So he, who wasn't even a Christian, was going to preach. I, meanwhile, who was a Christian, got to be a gofer. There was a kind of poetic justice in that setup that reminded me of too many things Jesus said. I couldn't fight it.

Omar tried to hide it, but the smug satisfaction was all over his face as he put the headset on.

# Chapter 4

At the Pittsburgh airport I got that tingling that told me we were being observed. Omar had his eyes open, but he was obviously looking for someone specific. He was letting me be the watchdog for general dangers. That was okay. If there's someone out there with hostile intentions toward me, I'd rather find him than have him find me.

We stopped at a newsstand and Omar searched the magazine racks until he found an issue of Charisma. It was right next to something about "Big Babes", so I figured it was a plant.

Since he was clearly about to make contact, and I could still feel the eyes out there somewhere, I said, "I'm gonna make a quick head call, Omar."

He nodded without looking up. "Good hunting."

So he felt it, too.

Turning from him, I saw a raincoat I'd noticed twice before. Could be coincidence. A lot of men wear raincoats, especially in autumn. But there was more. It was the same slightly stooped, hurried walk. It was the same studied care to not look back at me.

Two women were going back and forth, pretending to window shop. One was the eye-catcher, and the other was made up to look invisible. It was easier for men, but the right women could get by with it also.

Unless you knew how to find them.

The women would have to wait, for now.

I found the men's room and stood outside, looking furtive. Then I went in. I slipped into the last stall, against the back wall of the long room. I closed the seat and stood on it, bending so I wouldn't be seen over the top.

I heard varied footsteps, varied sounds, and was able to follow the guys I couldn't see from their entrance through hand washing and exit.

One came in and seemed to spend a long time at the urinals, because I heard an older gent mutter about perverts on his way out. Then he spent a longer time at the sinks. I guess he was trying out different hairstyles at the mirror.

His moment came. He was alone, so he started trying the doors to all the stalls, starting predictably with the first one.

I was ready for him. I pulled the door open just as he touched it and pulled him in. I knocked his head against the wall enough to daze him. While he shook his head, I patted him down and took his .38 away.

He noticed it pointing at him and froze.

"Strip," I said.

"What?"

"You heard me. The clothes. Off."

"Hey, I'm not into that..."

"Don't be funny!" I tapped the side of his head and rocked him.

I was really being gentle with him, so I guess he must have read my dossier. His eyes got big, and he started to shake and unbutton his shirt clumsily, staring at his gun in my hand.

We had good fortune. No one came in while he undressed. I bundled his clothes under one arm and stepped out of the stall. "You can close your door now," I said, smiling.

He did so without comment.

Then I stepped to the door and unloaded the gun, leaving it in the middle of the floor. Outside the restroom, I let the clothes drop from my hand against the wall and strode back to the newsstand.

Omar had made contact. He was talking to a well-dressed black man. They seemed to be getting along well.

Omar looked up and smiled. "Hey, Bill! This is Bishop Josh Wilson of the Upper Room Fellowship. We have a speaking engagement in his church tonight. Bishop, this is the man I've been telling you about."

He was telling this guy about me?

The Bishop smiled and held out his hand. "It's a pleasure to meet you, Brother Bill."

I took the hand and smiled back at him. "It's mutual, Bishop. I hope Omar didn't make me look too bad."

His eyes grew and he chuckled. "Quite the contrary! He told me about that spiritual warfare down in the Caribbean. Very impressive!"

Now I was really confused. The term "spiritual warfare" reminded me of some of the passages in the New Testament I'd read down there, but I still didn't really know what that was all about. Besides, that remark of his was too close to the truth. Omar didn't know the details himself, so I wasn't sure what this man thought I'd done.

"Well," I said, groping for words and praying silently at the same time, "it's really just a matter of stepping aside and letting God do it."

It must have been the right thing to say, because he nodded. "Doesn't it all really boil down to that? Anyway, let's not just stand here. I've got a car waiting to take you to your motel."

A motel sounded wonderful, but I just nodded.

Omar brightened at that also. "Lead on, Bishop. We're about ready for some rest and freshening before tonight."

We walked together, past the men's room that was now the scene of curiosity as two policemen examined the pile of clothes and another listened to an older man telling of what he'd seen and heard inside. The women stood together, looking confused, and glared at me as we passed them.

On the way to the car, the Bishop kept up a running monologue. "Our church started out three years ago with just my family. When we hooked up with Operation Blessing and started the food and blanket distribution, people started coming to our home Bible studies. Pretty soon we outgrew our home and had to rent a storefront. Now we're in an old warehouse, but it's been fixed up pretty good. We're averaging about five hundred on Sunday mornings now. I hope to have that doubled by next year. I'm getting them used to having two services, but so far it's just been vision casting, you know? We're starting strategic level warfare, too. We just started prayer walks in the neighborhood, and a few of the sisters have begun spiritual mapping. It's getting exciting to be on the front lines!"

Well, he was sure excited about it, though he'd left me in the dust somewhere around having two services.

"Sounds great!" I said, hoping it sounded sincere. "Any traditional street preaching being done?"

He rolled his eyes. "More than ever! Half a dozen brothers and sisters just love getting in people's faces with the Gospel! You'll meet them tonight. They'll probably try to get you to go out with them."

"That's great!" Omar said, grinning. "Bill's really into that!"

# Chapter 5

The motel room was clean and quiet. I took a quick shower and settled down for a nap while Omar took his turn.

When he stepped out, I said, "So you want me to hit the streets? I thought I was just a gofer on this case."

He looked surprised. "'Gofer'! Oh no, Bill. You're much more important to me than a gofer. You're...well, you're bait."

"I'm not sure if that's a step up or down."

"And I can't answer that; only you can. You see, this guy isn't interested in me at all. He wants you to find him. Even though I'm the one who's officially on assignment here, you're the crucial player."

I let my head drop back to the pillow. "I wonder why the strategic geniuses in Washington didn't figure that out?"

"Oh, now you want me to give one of those 'not for us to question why' speeches. No way, Bill. You know the answer to that as well as I do. You have suddenly become unreliable. You could have dispatched Ninshka the last time you left him. It was your new pacifistic tendencies that got us into this mess, so you are now considered a loose cannon...except it's not that they're afraid you'll fire in the wrong direction. They know you probably won't fire at all, and we'll be sorry for it again."

"So, what's the game plan?"

"There isn't one, yet. I'm an evangelist; you're my administrator and bottle washer. Our job is to be as conspicuous as possible among these holy types, and hope Ninshka is watching and makes a move on us."

"Some hope."

"Hey, it's no worse than your kamikaze stunt down in Haiti. You, Mr. Donley, are in no position to complain."

I shook my head. "I keep forgetting it was you down there. Are you sure you're really Omar?"

"You talk about other people changing!" He shook his head, laughed, and started to dress. "Well, we have a dinner date before the meeting, so you better get ready. Oh, and come up with something to share at these meetings, okay?"

"Something to share? The only meetings I've been to in the past month were with Chase or with the voodoo cult! What do you and this bishop mean by 'something to share'?"

"Oh, talk about a Bible verse, or how God helped you stop being so selfish and stupid. You know, things like that."

I sneered at him. "Yeah, things like that."

"Well, anyway, I have to get ready. They'll be here for us pretty soon, so you better be 'dressed and blessed' when they get here."

"I think I liked the West Indian Omar better."

"He's gone, friend. Long gone. I kind of liked him, too, but it's no longer his time."

I was getting up to find something to wear when the phone rang. Omar stopped and looked at me. Unsure of the protocol, I said, "Do you really want me to be the one they talk to first?"

"Hmm, I see your point." He closed the distance in three strides and picked up the receiver. "God bless you, this is Omar Jumbaya. How may I help you? Yes, yes, praise the Lord, we're almost ready." He made motions to hurry me along. "Of course, brother. Come right up." With that, he hung up.

We finished dressing in silence and were ready just as a timid knock sounded at the door.

I let them in. Two black men, conservatively dressed, with smiles and warm handshakes. The older said, "God bless you, brothers. Bishop Wilson sent us. I'm Bishop Standish, and this is Elder McBride. We thank God that you and Brother Jumbaya are able to share with us tonight."

Omar stepped out of the bathroom, beamed and boomed, "And so do we, Bishop, so do we!"

I tried to smile, but it was hard. Omar wasn't going to make this easy for me.

McBride seemed to be studying me. "I hear you've had a real run-in with the enemy, brother Donley."

Okay, so I was using my own name again. That suited me fine. I glanced at Omar for guidance, and he nodded. "Down in Haiti, brother. Go on and testify, Bill. You had a real encounter with those voodoo devils down there. Don't share the people's secrets, now. Just about the Lord's victory."

Hmm. I wasn't sure I liked using the real thing to get over on people like this, but I didn't have a better plan, and the truth was something I was trying to stick with anyway. I nodded. "I'm not sure American Christians are really ready for that kind of thing, actually."

"Ready for it!" the bishop roared. At least, it felt like he did to my ears. It seemed to me that the volume of this conversation was hitting decibel level. "It's right here, on our own streets and behind the closed curtains! Just open any newspaper. You'll see that the devil is alive and well in Pittsburgh, Pennsylvania! We need to hear about it, and we need to know what to do about it, whether we're ready for it or not. I want my people to fight the enemy instead of always getting stomped by him, so don't you hold anything back, y'hear?"

"Yes sir," I said, trying to sound meekly enthused. It was going to be a long night.

# *Chapter 6*

We heard the place long before we reached it. I was amazed the neighbors didn't call the cops. I heard the bass, then the drums, and when we got out of the car a wall of sound assaulted me that sounded disturbingly like the Haitian rhythm.

I looked up and down the block. It was crowded with rundown buildings. People were passing by, most of them ignoring the event. Occasionally someone on a stoop across the street would get up and start to dance, but someone else would say something and he or she would stop. Several windows had people leaning their elbows on the sills, listening and weaving as well as they could.

But the men with me were already bobbing to the beat. "Let's go have church!" Bishop Standish enthused.

It was a vacant lot, with a large tent erected on it. It reminded me of pictures of the old circuses. As we stepped under the flap, Omar had my ear alone for a second and muttered, "In the immortal words of Fats Waller, 'this joint is jumpin'.'"

And it was. The band was on a stage, giving it all they had. The choir was jumping, and people in the aisles were dancing. It wasn't the sensuous kind of modern dancing, or the partners-on-the-floor kind of the war years. This was a kind of double-time two-step, with arms waving.

But the joint was definitely jumping.

We were ushered onto the wooden stage and placed before chairs, but we weren't expected to sit on them. Our two hosts started doing the step immediately, but Omar knelt in front of his chair and maintained a praying posture. I decided that was the safest route for me and followed his example.

The difference was, I really prayed.

"Lord, what do I do with this? I'd almost rather be facing an enemy than going cold into a culture I don't understand. Most of these people are no doubt sincere, so let me somehow encourage them, without becoming part of the sham."

The words of the song started to penetrate. The leader was singing, "Whose report you gonna receive?"

The people shouted, "The Lord's report! The Lord's report!"

The leader refrained, with a slight change: "Whose report you gonna believe?"

The people repeated, "The Lord's report! The Lord's report!"

Out of the corner of my eye, I saw Omar get to his feet and start jumping with the rest of them. That made me feel like a neon placard was hanging around me, blinking "MISFIT" in alternating colors.

Mercifully, the music stopped. Thunderous applause and shouts of "Hallelujah!" and "Praise the Lord!" filled the air as everyone on stage took seats. I got off my knees and sat, gratefully.

Bishop Wilson jumped onto the stage. I hadn't seen him dancing until then. He had already worked up a sweat, but he didn't look ready to slow down. He grabbed a mike and said, "The devil is ma-ad...and I'm so-o-o-o glad!"

The crowd roared again at that.

"And speaking of that, we have a special guest here tonight who made the devil very upset recently."

A few oohs, ah's and other remarks, more subdued this time, but sounding impressed, greeted that statement.

"He travels with Brother Omar. He was trapped in the jungles of Haiti, by voodoo devil worshipers."

A collective gasp went up.

"And he is living proof that the Bible speaks truly when it says, 'Many are the afflictions of the righteous..."

A hum went up from the crowd at that.

"But the Lord..."

They got louder...

"Delivers him..."

...louder yet...

"...out...of...them...all'!"

This received a standing ovation and even a few bars from the band. While all that was going on, the Bishop caught my eye, grinned and beckoned me over. Feeling like I was heading for a firing squad, I got up, took a sweaty hug from the Bishop and was handed the microphone.

And again, I marveled at how affected I was. I'd stood in front of crowds and pretended to be all kinds of people, without missing a beat. But now I was telling half-truths in the name of a truth I embraced, for a mixed cause that I wasn't quite comfortable with.

"My name is Bill Donley," I started. So far, so good. "I can't really tell you why I was there, except that I was helping somebody. The rest of it is their story."

Yeah, "theirs". Chase's, the Secretary of Defense's, and the federal government's.

I heard a chorus of "That's all right", and "You go on and tell it, son, that's okay," and like that.

"I learned that I can be like a child, even in the face of demons."

Some chuckles greeted me now, and supportive calls from the congregation stayed with me.

"I can stand in the middle of a room full of demons, and still say, 'My Daddy can beat up your daddy'!"

I had to stop again. The crowd and the band responded.

"I was tied up, and forced to watch a human sacrifice. All I could think of to do was pray. And the Lord gave me a way out.

"The way was not according to any wisdom or strategy that would make sense. In fact, it sounded foolish even to me at the time, but I had no choice. I started to sing a song, a song my mother taught me when I was little, and it caused so much havoc and confusion that I was able to get myself and my friend away safely."

When the applause died down, the Bishop shouted, "What was the song?" and started others asking.

A warm encouragement spread out from a place deep within me, and I knew what I had to do. I gulped, swallowed, took a breath, and dove in. "It's a simple song; a childhood song, and it goes like this - Jesus loves me, this I know..."

The whole room immediately joined me. They stood, they raised their hands, and a lot of them swayed, but it was a moment of adoration like I'd never known before. I felt like I was ready to pass out, but I stood there and luxuriated in it, like a hot shower after a hard workout...but much deeper.

Then the people started singing something I couldn't figure out. It had no melody I could find, and everyone was singing different words, but it filled the tent with a kind of harmony I'd never heard before.

I took advantage of that to turn, find my chair and sit down heavily, feeling strangely exhausted.

Omar had the mike now, and everyone was sitting again. "You know," he was saying, "I love Brother Bill, but I wish he wouldn't steal my fire like that!"

They laughed.

"Turn with me in your Bibles to Acts, chapter 10, verse 38." He waited through all the page turning. "Peter is preaching the Gospel to Gentiles for the first time ever, and he says this: '...how God anointed Jesus of Nazareth with the Holy Spirit and with power, who went about doing good and healing all who were oppressed by the devil, for God was with Him.'"

He looked around the room slowly with a stern authority. He was good. I almost believed him.

"Now, for you theologians here tonight..." scattered laughter greeted this. "We can see the Trinity in this verse. There's God the Father, there's Jesus who is God the Son, and the Holy Ghost!

"But the first active word...I mean the first practical word...the first word that gets the blood pumpin' and the feet movin', is that word, 'anointed'."

"Jesus was anointed! Before He could do any of the things we remember from the Bible, He was anointed!"

This received a shout and a clap.

"So, before we can do anything for God-ah, we've got to get into His presence. We've got to get down on our knees. We've got to cry out and say, 'God, I need your anointing!'"

It went on like that for almost an hour. Omar worked up a respectable sweat and the congregation nearly worked themselves into a froth. I tried to act like I was involved, laughing, nodding and so forth. But actually, I was searching the tent and trying to see into the darkness beyond it, looking for the anomaly; the person or thing that didn't fit.

Patience rewarded me. I saw two men pacing in the back and up and down the side aisles like monitors. They weaved in and out of standing-room-only worshipers, but the pattern emerged. Like me, they made a pretense of involvement, but they were really just watching.

Watching me.

Omar was winding up. "Some of you here tonight need a touch from the Lord. Some of you need to be healed. Some of you need to be delivered. Some of you didn't plan to be here tonight, but the Holy Ghost brought you, and you need to get saved. Others just want a touch from Jesus. I'm going to call you now to be honest and step to the front so we can pray for you."

The band had been quietly taking their places, and they started playing "Jesus Loves Me" softly behind him.

Then people all over the room started getting out of the seats and heading toward us. Some were weeping, and some were shaking for some reason. I completely lost track of the two watchers in the sea of humanity.

Then Omar and the Bishop were beckoning me off the stage, so I rose and followed...to find myself facing a line of people. The Bishop leaned into my ear and whispered, "These people were moved by your talk, so they want you to be the one who prays for them."

"Me?"

"God blessed your words. Now He'll bless your prayers."

Well, I couldn't argue with that. But I still didn't know what to say or how to begin. I watched the Bishop and Omar. They each put a hand on the person's forehead, closed their eyes and began praying out loud with gusto.

I turned to the first in line. There stood a middle-aged woman with a tear in her eye. "I've lost my childlike faith," she said, softly, "and I want it back."

That seemed easy enough. I put my hand on her forehead like the others and said, "God..." and suddenly she wasn't there anymore.

I opened my eyes and found her on the ground at my feet, weeping and laughing at the same time. She was muttering, "Jesus...I love You, Jesus..."

I thought, "That's it?" but since nobody seemed to think that was unusual, I looked at the next one. This was a young, well-dressed man. "I have sin in my life," he whispered, "and I want to get right with God."

"Well, let's pray," I said. Before I could say anything, he started to cry and said, "Oh, God, I'm sorry, I'm sorry, I'm sorry..." and sank to his knees right there.

That kind of thing went on for over an hour. I barely got a word in edgewise, which was all right with me. Mentally thanking God for working it out like this, I tried to keep an eye out for the watchers, but they had either left or they were keeping to the back.

The music began to change after a while, getting more up-tempo. The people responded, swaying and dancing as they waited for prayer. One young woman started to bounce up and down after I touched her, and kept it up, eyes closed rapturously, while two other women kept an eye on her and moved some of the folding chairs out of the way.

Then the music mellowed out again, and I looked for the next one in line to find nobody standing there. A few were still lying on the ground, but the only standing people were collecting their Bibles and slipping out.

Bishop Standish was wiping his brow, smiling. "Praise the Lord, what a night of glory! Bill, I thought I'd made a mistake when you first got up there; you looked like a nervous wreck, you know what I'm sayin'? But you sure have the power, brother! And Omar, you preached up a storm! You two chased the devils off this street tonight!

"Well, like the Bible says, 'the laborer is worthy of his hire'. Let's get you two fed and back to your room!"

Food sounded great to me. I was exhausted and hungry, even though we'd eaten on our way here.

Omar was quiet. He looked kind of troubled.

# Chapter 7

We ate at a Denny's, all of us eating breakfast-type food. The Bishop did most of the talking, which was fine. It was an education in the kinds of things that can happen when you pray for people in situations like that. I couldn't help but feeling "I hope we find Ninshka soon!"

Back at the motel, I beat Omar to the bathroom and was ready for bed while he went in. I was just drifting off to sleep when he said, "Bill?"

Swallowing my annoyance, I said, "Hmm?"

"What'd you think of it all?"

"I'm afraid to try thinking about it." I muttered, fluffing my pillow, turning over and trying to hint.

"No, I mean, really. You're into this stuff; I'm not. I feel all out at sea here. What was it about?"

That made me sit up. "You looked a lot more 'into' it than I was."

He grunted. "Not from where I stood."

"Hey, I was saved in a shack in Bulgaria. Then I was immediately thrown into your loving embrace. I haven't even been to church yet...unless tonight counts."

"I'm sure it does."

"Maybe. It was certainly better than those old 'three hymns and a responsive reading' sessions I remember from other churches I've been to. There was something...I don't know, something wrong about it somehow. I'm sure some of those people got hold of something very real tonight, but it wasn't from us. As for the rest, it was like the accent was on showbiz instead of truth."

"Yeah, I know what you mean..."

I think he would have gone on in that vein, but I wanted to talk about something else first. "Did you see the watchers in the crowd?"

He nodded. "They looked like Mormons. All they needed was the nametags. When the ministry started, they looked uncomfortable. I tried to keep an eye on them, but then I had to focus on trying to look like I knew what I was doing, so I lost track of them."

"Me, too. I think if I see them again, I'm going to step out for a few minutes and see what they do."

"That's dangerous, man. I'll be stuck up front, and we don't have backup. What'll you do if they start something?"

"The same thing I did to Jardine. I'm not helpless, you know. And, after all, I am supposed to be bait. That's my whole function in this. What good is bait if you don't dangle it?"

"You have a point there, Bill. I almost forgot about that, I'm having so much fun."

At first I glared at him, then saw the grin and couldn't help smirking. That got him chuckling, which started me off. In a few minutes, we were both laughing hysterically at ourselves. I stood up and struck the pose he'd done several times, Bible up in the air and other hand pointing into the crowd. "The Lord-ah! Said to me-ah!"

Omar said, "Yeah! The Lord say-ed, 'Sit down and shut up!'"

We went on like that for a few minutes. Then it wore off and we were very quiet, trying to process it all.

"Bill, I have a terrible feeling we're living in two different worlds at the same time."

I nodded. "I know that one well. I've felt like that since Bulgaria."

He looked like he wanted to say more, then changed his mind and got ready for bed. I was suddenly sorry I'd interrupted him to talk business, even though it was a life and death kind of business.

I slumped in a prefabricated chair and pulled out my pocket Bible. Finding the Book of Acts, I read the whole tenth chapter to make sure Omar had been talking about the right thing. I still wasn't sure.

When he stepped out of the bathroom I said, "You didn't just make up that message tonight, did you?"

He snorted and said, "Remember those tapes I've been listening to?"

"Oh."

"Yeah. You know, I've spent a lot of time conning a lot of people. I believe it's been for a good cause, but right now...for the first time...I don't feel so good about it. They were getting something from somewhere, and it sure wasn't from me. Meanwhile, I was right in the middle of it, missing out! I sure hope your boy makes his move soon, Bill."

"Yeah, me, too."

And what about Carmen? Was she still alive? Was she still safe? Was she driving Ninshka as crazy as she drove me? Would he put up with it, or do something drastic? These questions were driving me crazy. There was no answer...not until I found them and we had our face-to-face. And right now, all we could do was wait for them to find us.

I was hoping they already had. I was hoping those men who didn't try very hard to hide were from him...but I just didn't know.

And Carmen's danger bothered me almost too much. I was beginning to worry about how I'd do with my emotions going the way they were. Chase's predicament hadn't bothered me this much. And if I successfully rescued her again, how would she feel? Would I still be the sleazeball she disapproved of? Would she just be happy I was saved and want to be brother and sister? I didn't think I could bear that...though I hadn't thought about it until now. I was hoping I'd find that out before the showdown.

But even that was unprofessional. I had to focus. This was already affecting my performance, and not for the better.

Lord, why now? Why couldn't we find out we belonged together at the same time, and after the danger is past? Help me, Lord. I'm afraid I'll make a bad judgment call because of the way I feel. I'm barely regaining my balance from being able to accept Your love. Now you've got me caring for someone who probably wouldn't care if she never saw me again.

And what is this crazy attraction that can be spiritual and emotional as well as physical, and yet be a clean thing without the guilty pleasure of lust?

I'm out of my depth again, *God. Help!*

# Chapter 8

It took Omar less than ten minutes to fall asleep. When I could hear his measured almost-snoring, I slipped out of bed and got dressed. Then I stepped out of the room and walked down the hall as if I knew where I was going.

Which, in a sense, I did. I crossed the lobby and stepped out the front door without trying to be subtle. Outside, I paced on the sidewalk for a while. If anyone was watching me, they were happy to stay out of sight. After about fifteen minutes I gave it up and stepped back inside.

I heard the noises from the motel's bar.

I'd forgotten the place even had one. I approached the glass window and looked in, trying to appear casual. It was dark, but there was enough light to see the people you were with. Neon signs advertising various brands of beer littered the walls, and it had a for-real jukebox playing oldies. Finally, I stepped in and ordered a beer. When I had it, I carried it around, checking out the pool game and several of the video games. Nobody seemed to be paying me much attention, so I put the glass down on an empty table and left.

It wasn't until I was in the corridor outside my room that I realized I wasn't alone. There were two of them, about ten paces behind me.

If I got into the room, Omar would be awake in a flash and at my side. The odds would be more even then, but I'd probably get nailed while fumbling with the lock. So I picked up my pace just a little and marched right past my room to the exit at the end of the hall.

Outside I ducked to the right and ran, keeping behind some tall bushes until I emerged into a parking lot behind the building. My pursuers had abandoned subtlety and were close behind me.

When the shadow seemed darkest, I turned and ran headlong into the first one, knocking the wind out of him. With him down for a moment, I concentrated on the second one.

He didn't want to play footsie. In his hand was a big .9 mm and he was raising it slowly, enjoying the frustration on my face. It was that moment of frustration that cost him. I went into a forward roll and came up under his gun hand. He tried to follow me, but I had his wrist in my hand and pulled it up as I came to my full height. Then I pushed it forward and down, which was backward for him.

The snap of his arm was loud. He squealed and fainted.

Number one was starting to rise, so I kicked his head against the wall of the building so he'd stay out for a while. He was going to need counseling, the way he was being neglected tonight.

That was fine with me. Anyway, I was tired. Omar was supposed to be the one working on this case. I'd had enough of doing his job...for one night. Maybe tomorrow I'd feel better about it.

Now Ninshka would know for sure. Without saying a word, I was sending him a response: Message received. I'm coming for you.

I wanted him to know he could feel free to send along any new clues he had waiting for me. Hopefully, he would be off-balance. This violence was not in the plan. Maybe I wasn't the pacifist he thought I was, after all.

I left the gun on the asphalt, slipped back inside and in minutes my head was on a pillow. I let sleep carry me away.

# *Chapter 9*

Omar woke me up at noon. "C'mon Bill. I'm getting hungry. Get up and let's go get some breakfast."

I sat up groggily. "Breakfast...yeah..." and stumbled into the shower...where I woke up.

There was a diner across the street, so we had greasy-spoon cholesterol specials and compared notes again.

After hearing about my escapades the night before, he shook his head. "You know, the weird thing is, I'd rather do that than stand up in front of those people and preach again."

"By the time this is over, I'm sure you'll get your chance. What's on the schedule for today?"

He sighed, "More preaching, teaching, praying and Bill-dangling."

"That's not until tonight. What about this afternoon?"

"You're kidding, right?" When I didn't answer, he went on, "I mean, don't you want to rest? You had a rough night, though it didn't seem as rough as mine...then you had a knock-down with some bad guys...all in all, you didn't get a lot of sleep. How about just taking it easy this afternoon?"

"Well...dangling's easy."

"You're just going to keep rubbing my face in that, aren't you?"

"Any reason I shouldn't?"

"Yeah, this religion of yours that's driving me crazy! You're supposed to love your neighbor, go the extra mile, stuff like that!"

"Hey, it's not like I'm the one who's being mean to you, you know! You're the one who's 'dangling' me, remember? Anyway, I'm not sleepy. I want to get this one over with."

"Yeah, so you can propose to your beloved Cuban damsel and ride off into the sunset."

My mind blanked out. I sat and stared at him while he grinned and shoveled home fries into his mouth.

When he'd swallowed, he picked up his coffee cup and chuckled. "It's a real comedy being with you, Bill. You're head over heels in love with this girl, and you don't even know it."

"You do? The ever-wise and knowledgeable Reverend Doctor Omar the Magnificent?"

That brought the desired wince, but it was a cheap victory and I knew it. "Ow! Touched a nerve there, did I?" He put his utensils down and his eyes bored into mine. "Well, you better get focused, Bill. If I can rattle you like that, what do you think this clown's going to do? You can't afford to lose control here, especially if there is something between you two."

He was right, and he knew it... He'd reached me where it hurt, and he knew that, too.

"I haven't been in contact with her since we separated in Greece. It was rather sudden. One of Chase's quick-changes." He nodded his understanding. "She's probably ticked off at me."

"That doesn't mean there isn't something there. In fact, it might mean there is, you know?"

"Well, we won't know about that until we see her, will we?"

"And maybe not even then, if her state of pathological denial's anything like yours."

I deflated. There wasn't really anything to defend, except my discomfort at being caught like that. I had some serious thinking to do...and it wouldn't get done with Omar sitting here making remarks at me. "So then, we just keep up the 'ol' time religion' until he makes his move? That's the whole plan?"

"We have had this conversation already, and you know the answer. We might have fun like you did last night, though it probably won't make things easier when the time comes."

"How about who they were?"

"Good point. They were probably registered in the motel, though under aliases. On second thought, the names they used here wouldn't mean anything."

"But then, it might tell us something."

"Then go look."

"I think I will."

"My brilliant mind says we just ought to be properly grateful that you were able to take them out of play and get on with the good fight."

I shook my head. "I don't like leaving loose ends. I might try to find an excuse to look in the register."

"Investigating that should give you something to do while I'm preparing tonight's message. Frankly, you could do some homework, too. They'll be expecting something after last night, and I don't think you have a whole lot to just throw out like that."

"I wouldn't even know where to begin."

"Begin with the Bible, Mister Christian! This is supposed to be your thing! That's the Book, or don't you remember? Find something to say a few words about, and you're home free! I have to fill up an hour or so, and make sense at that! Plus, it has to be exciting."

"You could just use your Berlitz 'Learn to Preach Overnight' tapes."

"Funny man. But I could feel the difference between us last night, Bill. I was doing the thing, and they responded to it because it's what they're used to, but you had something real. What you did was clumsy and unpolished, but it was real. You connected with them, and there was a kind of electricity, even when you were praying for them later, that seemed to spill over onto the sham that I was doing. I can't help but feel that I would have gone bust last night if you hadn't been there. See if you can work on that somehow. It...it might, well, help somebody somehow. It would...well...oh, I don't know."

Strangely, I was warmed and encouraged by that speech. And he was right. I should take this more seriously. If I were posing as a mechanic, I'd be puttering around with engines and such. Well, this wasn't supposed to be a pose. I was a Christian; a Christian who'd been through some things. Maybe I couldn't preach, but I should have something to say.

And, I was still hungry. "Okay, it's homework time." And with that, I attacked the rest of my plate.

"Good. I have a million questions about this Bible of yours, and I'm hoping for some lucid answers."

# Chapter 10

ack at the motel room, we had our Bibles and notebooks open, and Omar was pacing. "So the Romanian kid couldn't finish the quote, and your girlfriend finished it for her without even looking it up?"

His use of the word "girlfriend" was offensive, but he wouldn't have cared. I let it go. "That's about it."

He thought about it, then shrugged. "There's nothing miraculous about being so familiar with the Bible that you know where certain verses are. Anybody who's enthused about anything gets knowledgeable about it."

My first reaction was to defend her, but I stopped in time to realize he wasn't attacking her. In fact, he was right.

"Okay," he said, "tell me more. What happened then?"

"So you just went sailing through the checkpoint while they chewed each other out about the booze, right?"

"Yeah, that's right."

"Well, that's impressive. It can be explained away, but I'm not sure I want to do that. It's too good as a miracle story to spoil with an explanation, you know?"

"I'm not sure an explanation would spoil it. Even if you could find some natural reason for it...and I told you how it happened, you can't get past the enormous coincidence that it happened just when it did."

"Except for that word you just used: 'coincidence'."

"That's a cop-out and we both know it."

He laughed. "Yeah, we both know it. Okay, talk to me some more. Then what happened?"

"So you called her father the 'smuggler's ransom', and she threw all these Bible verses about Jesus ransoming her at you?"

"I'm not trying to make anything out of that, but you wanted to know what happened."

"That's okay. This is all helping me understand. Then you fell asleep and remembered your mom."

"It was the first time I couldn't stop the memories once they started."

"Yeah, yeah. So Carmen triggered something that your Mom put in you a long time ago." He shook his head and chuckled ruefully. "You know, it really is kind of too bad this all snapped together for you when it did. If you'd found religion just one day later, we wouldn't be having this problem."

"Well, I didn't plan it. None of this happened according my timetable. In fact, if it had been up to me, it never would have happened, period."

"Yeah, I know. I'm not criticizing. Anyway, you prayed to get saved, and then this dirtbag busted in on you?"

"Like clockwork."

"I can see why you didn't plan it that way."

That was gratifying, in a way, but I didn't get to answer it. The Bishop and the Elder showed up and it was time to go.

I still hadn't prepared anything.

# *Chapter 11*

The music had been loud and long. Omar had worked up a sweat along with the Bishops and Deacon. Even I got up when I didn't feel so silly about it. Mostly I stayed kneeling at my chair, praying fervently and sincerely. God, is this real? Is this something I should get comfortable with? Help me know where all this fits in with my future. In Jesus' Name, Amen.

In all of that, I forgot to pray about what I would say.

Then the moment came. It was Bishop Standish this time, and he introduced me as "the disciple whom Jesus loves" and everyone laughed.

As I stood up and reached for the mic, a wave of calm and confidence went over me and I looked out over the crowd. The middle-aged, mostly black women seemed to be more visible than the other people in the seats, somehow. Suddenly I knew that I had something to share.

"How many mothers are here tonight?" I decided to ask it that way to get them involved. This was something I wanted to reach them with. It worked. Hands went up all over the place. "I want to tell you a little bit about mine. I don't remember much about my mother. But I remember that she told me about Jesus, and I remember that she prayed for me.

"She died when I was about twelve, and that made me angry at God. For sixteen years I lived a life that I knew would not please Him, and gave me a perverse kind of gratification. He finally caught up with me, in a foreign country. He sent me to a faithful witness, and even though I didn't want to be reminded, He didn't let me escape from my mother's prayers.

"How many of you mothers here tonight are praying for someone you care about?"

I thought maybe half the hands would go up. I was surprised again. Just about every one of those who'd raised them before sent them up again. Most of them were crying.

"Why don't you stand up right now, and I'll pray for you. Then, if you want more prayer, Brother Omar will pray for you again later."

Folding chairs were slid back and women stood up all over the room. I was on automatic pilot. I had no idea what I was going to say, but I wasn't worried about it for some reason.

I opened my mouth to pray and words came out.

"Father, I hold up these mothers before You tonight. Some of their hearts are already broken. Some of them may never see the answers to their prayers, like mine didn't. I want to pray that You give them peace in their hearts, and determination to never give up praying for their children. Give them a backbone of steel to stick with it and to know You're in charge, and You won't let their rebellious children keep it up forever; You'll chase them down and put Your foot on their necks and make them yield their lives to You."

The people responded, but my memory of exactly what happened after that is a blur. I don't remember what I said or what happened, except that it was an overall positive experience for everyone.

While the Bishop introduced Omar, I slipped off the platform and out from under the tent. I slowly circled the structure, watching for more watchers.

Some of the neighbors were out again, listening from safely across the street, sitting on stoops and drinking beer. There was a folding table outside a grocery store on the corner to our left. Three men were seated, playing cards or dominoes or something.

After I checked out the neighborhood, I slipped into the tent behind the last row of seats. It took a while, but I found both of them before they figured out where I was. Their confusion gave them away. They must have thought I was going to the john or something when I left. Now I hadn't returned, and they weren't sure what to do.

Omar was preaching up a storm, but I didn't listen this time. I knew it was just a rehash of someone else's hype. Besides, I had dangling to do. One of them turned around and saw me. I reacted like I didn't want that and stepped back out of the tent. I saw him trying to catch the other one's eye, finally succeed, and signal for them both to follow me.

Good. Sharks coming for the bait.

Not that I had much respect for them as sharks. Real pros would have been much harder to find or lure. These two, like last night's, seemed to be purely local muscle. Ninshka couldn't import his help this time. He had to settle for local lowlifes. He really was "persona non grata". I didn't want to hurt these guys too much, but I could still use them to send another message.

I slipped over to the sidewalk, ran past a few doors, and stepped into an alley between buildings. I had to step carefully around garbage bags and discarded furniture. Once the shadows were dark enough, I crouched and waited.

They were good at this kind of thing. They didn't panic and run, as I'd hoped. They took their time. My legs cramped as I counted off the seconds for their arrival.

One of them finally showed up, moving slowly and carefully. I moved the garbage can I was behind slightly, just enough to draw his attention. He reacted, then stood very still, listening for another sound.

Making another at this point would have advertised that I wanted him to come in. I stayed silent.

He kept waiting.

Then, ever so faintly, I let my breath out, as if in pain.

He heard it and was encouraged. He stepped inside, moving away from the glare of the streetlight and into the shadow so his eyes could adjust to the darkness of the alley.

But I didn't want to give him that much time. I picked up a brick and silently pitched it at his head, praying it wouldn't be a lethal blow. It made contact and he crumbled with a grunt.

I was at his side, riffling through his pockets when his partner came into view. Fortunately, he was across the street.

I was happy to notice that my victim was still breathing. There was no identification, which didn't surprise me. He had a pistol tucked into his belt at the small of the back. Not even a speed rig. This was bargain basement muscle. In the dark, I could only tell that it was a double-action revolver. It didn't matter, since I had no intention of using it.

With him unconscious and disarmed, I was ready for Phase Two. I kicked the garbage can over and stepped right inside the shadow, flat against the wall of the building.

That brought the partner running across the street, stopping at the mouth of the alley. "Toby?" he whispered. "You get him, Toby?"

I let the silence fill the next few moments. Trying to answer might put him off his guard, but I had no assurance that his friend's name was really Toby. Besides, I didn't know what his voice sounded like, or if he had an accent. I could be digging my own grave saying anything, so I kept my mouth shut.

As he went to reach for his own piece, I leaped across the distance between us and grabbed his wrist, twisting it around so his arm was up behind him, painfully.

"Toby bit the dust, and you'll join him if I don't believe what I hear," I hissed into his ear.

He stiffened, then relaxed. He would play along, until he could think of something to do.

"First question. What's your boss' name these days?"

"He said it was...it was Ian...Ian Ludlum."

"Yeah, sure! Why not Mickey Chandler or Rex Parker?"

He squirmed and said, "Hey look, I...I don't believe it, either. That ain't even a cute fake, b...but his cash is green, man."

"You'll be a green man in a minute. Where is he?"

He stiffened again, so I pushed his hand closer to his neck. He groaned. "He's...he's up in the north country. He's not hidin' from you, man. You don't have to do this."

"Well, if you're all so friendly, why didn't you just come up and tell me where to go."

"I'd like to tell you where to..."

The hand went a millimeter higher.

"He's...he's in Bradford County. Small town called Ephesus. There's a retreat center there. It's all set up. You're goin' there to talk to a group called the Gospel Outreach. He'll be waitin'."

"And the girl?"

"What gir...ow!"

I wasn't about to put up with that nonsense. There wasn't time. I didn't have to say anything. He started blabbering again.

"She's there, man! She's bein' watched, but she's not tied up or nothin'. He's takin' care of her, makin' sure she's not hurt or nothin'...at least until you get there."

"Okay, thanks. Tell him I said I'll see him soon."

I let his wrist go.

He brought it around front and was ready to follow through with a kick or a chop, but he never made it, because I hit him on the head with the butt of his buddy's revolver.

# *Chapter 12*

The rest of the week became a routine. Omar became quieter and more uncomfortable with each night. On Thursday, the Bishop told us that a missionary training outfit called Gospel Outreach had called and wanted us to come for a week and train their students. Omar looked uncertain, but I knew this was what we were waiting for and accepted with enthusiasm.

So we finished up on Friday, with no more watchers bothering us, and packed our things when we got back to the room. Early the next morning, Bishop Standish came to take us back to the airport.

At the airport I saw the two women again. I couldn't figure out if they were friends or foes. The place was too crowded for me to make a good assessment of the number of other possible watchers before we had to get on the puddle jumper to Williamsport.

The Williamsport excuse for an airport was even smaller than the Kingston airport in the Bahamas...and Kingston had less land to work with. The good part was we made it through baggage claims and to the parking lot in record time.

I was used to working with only "need to know" information. It was frustrating at the best of times, but this knowing nothing routine was getting very old very fast.

Omar stood still, letting his gaze scan the lot. I could tell he was looking for a specific car. He seemed to be getting antsy as he searched among the dozen or so cars a second time.

"I can see the car you're looking for isn't here," I commented, "so maybe it's time for Plan B."

He looked like he was going to make a smart remark at me, but he suddenly found something on the road approaching the lot. I followed his gaze and saw a long white and grey van, with the words "GLOBAL OUTREACH" in stylized lettering on the side. It was putt-putting down the road slowly, almost painfully. A real hot-rodder, this was.

Omar smiled. "That's our ride, Bill. I've been told you Christians are about half an hour behind the rest of us. Now I see it in action."

I didn't know whether he meant their lateness or speed, and I didn't bother trying to find out. After all, I was just a tag-along.

Correction: I was the dangling bait.

A young woman stepped out of the van and smiled at us. "Brothers Omar and Bill?"

We nodded.

"Hi, I'm Beth Grenshacki. Let's get your stuff on board and then we can head north, to the Center."

"Sounds like we're going to cross the Arctic Circle," Omar commented.

She laughed. "It feels like that sometimes, too!"

The rear seat had been removed. It was easy to throw our bags into the back end, slam the door, then clamber into the side door while she started the engine and pulled onto the road.

I wanted to enjoy the scenery, but Omar was still giving the whole world the silent treatment. Sociability was my job this time. "So, what have the students been learning so far?"

She brightened and started reporting with gusto. "Oh, we learned how to forgive and get healed of the past, and...we learned the Father Heart of God, why God's heart has always been toward all the nations, and not just Israel...that was a good one! That teacher went through the whole Bible to show us that. I always thought the Old Testament was just about Israel, but now I know better. It was intense. Now we're up to you! What'll you teach?"

Omar muttered, "miracles", and I blurted, "confronting demons" at the same time. Her eyes grew and she said, "Wow..." and drove in silence for a while.

In spite of the faux pas, I really did enjoy the scenery. It was hilly and heavily wooded, dotted with farmland. The little towns we passed through were picturesque, but didn't look very prosperous. There were deserted barns, falling apart with peeling ads on the side. One said, "CHEW REDM..."and made me wonder if they were really that friendly to the Bible around here, or was it redneck country?

One town seemed to have a church on every corner. I took it as an opportunity to comment, "They sure seem friendly to God around here."

She noticed where I was looking and said, "Not really. They're religious, but they don't know the Lord. It's all just tradition with these people. 'Don't rock the boat, even if God says to', kind of thing. I'd rather deal with sleazy non-Christians than those people."

I wondered what she'd think if she knew the truth about the school's new guest speakers.

Omar thought of something practical to ask. "Anybody else using the place this week?"

She nodded. "It's also a retreat center, so there's another building that other groups can use, even during schools. It's called the 'Elijah House', and it's down the hill and across the road. There's a group there this week. They're some kind of Christian militia, having a time of seeking God."

Omar and I exchanged a look. "Christian militia? Sounds kind of...well... subversive, you know?"

She laughed. "Yeah, I thought so, too, when I first heard about them. But they're really very nice, and they do know the Lord. They're just concerned that the government might come and take their kids away...it's been happening, you know? So, they're getting ready to defend their families. It's in the Constitution that they can do that, even though the government doesn't like it. I forget where, but they know all about it. Maybe they'll let you speak to them, too!"

"I hope so!" I said, thinking about how nice it would be to have an army at my back. I also intended to visit them and discuss this pacifist question that was so crucial to Carmen.

Omar looked troubled again and stared out his window without saying anything. That was fine with me. I decided to enjoy my own window again. The scenery was nice, if a little uniform. It was calendar-picture, classic, rustic America...though I hoped I'd never have to live day-by-day in it.

We finally turned off Route 14 onto a dirt road that wound up the side of a mountain. I wasn't sure the huge 15-passenger van would make it. "Is this thing usually full when you take it up here?" I asked.

"Not usually, but it makes it without any trouble. Except in winter, that is. The ice can keep anything from getting up here."

"Well, I'm glad it's not winter!" Omar said.

I kept quiet, though I was thinking about some times when I had wished nobody could get up the hill to me.

The van pulled around the big building and into a small gravel parking lot that had railroad ties on the ground to show its perimeter. Two enthusiastic young men were waiting for us. They introduced themselves the minute we stepped out of the van. I promptly forgot their names. Quickly and efficiently, they took our luggage and led us around to the front, up a flight of stairs, through the front doors and around some turns to a suite of rooms. "This one's for Brother Omar..." one of the young men said. "We usually try to put teams close together. Our instructions were to put Bill at the end of the hall this time. I hope that's okay."

Wondering whose instructions they were following, I said, "It's fine. Where is it?"

One of the others said, "Right down here. Follow me." We took a left in the hall and went to the end, right by the exit door. My room was on the left, on the same side as Omar's. It was homey, in an old-world kind of way. There was a single bed against one wall, a dresser and a small writing table. The bed was covered with clashing quilts and a framed embroidery on the wall said, "Behold, I send you forth as lambs among wolves..."

When I closed the door, a poster greeted me with a painting of a lion with a crown, and the caption read "The Lion of Judah".

So, here I was in a room full of lambs, wolves and lions. It seemed appropriate, somehow.

The printed schedule on the writing table said dinner would be in two hours. I stepped into the lounge area, asked for a wake-up, returned to my room and promptly crashed.

Or tried to.

The knock at my door came just as I felt the curtain of sleep closing over my mind. I shook my head and muttered, "Come in," expecting to see an over eager student.

Omar stepped in the room and closed the door behind him. He grabbed the chair and sat down.

# Chapter 13

"**I** been shot at, stabbed, punched, kicked and left for dead," he said. "I've even been in situations where my cover was blown. But they never bothered me like this one, Bill. This place isn't like in Pittsburgh. It isn't just some revival meeting. These people expect to hear something with substance, and I don't have a thing to give them. It shouldn't bother me this much; it's not even why we're here. I'm a nervous wreck over this thing. I can't bear the thought that they'll know how phony I am."

I raised myself on one elbow, hoping this wouldn't last long. "Well, you have a few choices. First, I know you've had your cover blown before, and you've lived to tell about it. You're not in immediate danger on this assignment; I am. So just wing it. Hold discussion groups instead of teachings. A group like this would probably love that. They'd take over on you. You'd just have to be referee. Or you could just come clean, up to a point. Tell them you'd be a hypocrite if you stayed and take off. After all, I'm the one Ninshka, a.k.a. Ludlum, wants. And I'm here. You can fade out now, if you want to."

He shook his head. "No, that wouldn't work. I'm still the only one officially on assignment here. Chase and the boys in D.C. know you're with me. You're necessary but unsanctioned, remember? Besides, I think you're deliberately misunderstanding me, aren't you?"

"Maybe."

He glared at me. Then his gaze hit the floor. "I can't get rid of the feeling that the only way justice could be served with me is in hell. That's where I deserve to go. That's hard, Bill. I've always seen myself as one of the good guys, saving the world from tyranny and all that. Now that all looks like a sham...like a way to get away with doing what's wrong. Suddenly nobody's as bad as me."

"Is that your only conclusion?"

"No, of course not. It's just...it's that...I just don't...Bill, is this the way it happened to you?"

I could have been cute and said, "The way what happened?" but he was too vulnerable, and I wasn't used to seeing him like that. It made me more than a little uncomfortable.

I had another idea. "Let's look in the Book," I said. "Got yours?"

He nodded, perfectly serious. His big, black leather Bible was in his right hand. My little pocket edition looked pathetic next to it.

"I've been reading recently in Romans." I said, "and I think it'll answer some of this for us."

We read and talked for about an hour. He saw me falling asleep against my own will and let himself out. At least, that's what I think happened. All I knew was that suddenly there was another knock on the door and the student was announcing dinner.

The cafeteria was downstairs. About twenty people were scattered around the tables. Some were talking quietly. Omar was seated already. It seemed they were waiting just for me. Then an older man stood up and said, "Jimmy, why don't you pray tonight?"

The student who'd just brought me down bowed his head and prayed, "Father, I thank You for this food, and for our new teachers. I pray you'll bless them this week and bless the food to our bodies now. In Jesus' Name, Amen."

A chorus of "amens" greeted that, and the older guy invited me to a place at his table, next to Omar.

The food was simple, but very tasty, if a bit heavy. This was "farmer food". I thought it was a good thing that most of the students were young enough that it wouldn't give them heart problems...yet.

"I'm Daniel Buschmann," our host said to me. "I apologize for not being here earlier to greet you. I'm glad you were able to get some rest."

I nodded with my mouth full. When I'd swallowed, I said, "It's a nice, comfortable place. And very quiet, after a week in Pittsburgh."

The conversation went on like that, inanities designed to get familiar. We played along, saying things loud enough so we'd each hear what the other was saying and not get caught in a contradiction. I managed to avoid outright lies, but I still didn't feel good about the impression I was giving them.

The meal ended and we slipped out in the confusion of cleaning up. Omar looked like he wanted to pick up our talk where we'd left it, but he let me take the lead. "Let's give everyone a half-hour or so, then wander into the meeting room. Just listening to them will probably help a lot."

He looked at me, like he was searching for something, then nodded silently and stepped into his "guest speaker's suite".

I had to chuckle. At this point, he was so churned up I think he'd have traded places with me. Dangling in front of killers apparently looked better than dangling in front of Christians.

But I was uncomfortable about him, too, and I knew it. I didn't know what to do about it. I knew what had happened to me, but I didn't know all the theology or answers to the kind of questions he had. I knew he was burning up inside and needed resolution. I felt like I was failing at something more important than the assignment. Possibly even more important than Carmen's life...though I didn't want to meditate on that one too long.

There was nothing in my room for me right then, so I wandered outside onto the porch. There were several rocking chairs. I eased into one and surveyed the hillside we were on. About fifty yards down the hill was the dirt road. On the other side, a huge house with all the windows lit up tickled my memory. Was that connected to this place? Was it...Then I remembered. Elijah House. The militia!

As I was making a mental note to talk to them when I could, I saw a form slip across the lawn, trying to be invisible in the gloom. It was heading away from the woods to the house where the director and his wife lived.

# Chapter 14

I knew I only had about twenty minutes before Omar would be expecting me, but I didn't think this little matter would wait. I thought about bringing him in on it, but I felt he had more important things on his mind right then.

I slipped off the porch and headed toward the left, away from the lights. Then I carefully stepped down the side of the slippery, freshly mown lawn to the far side of the house. It was actually the front. A driveway went past the front porch and back to the dirt road. To my right was an addition that held an office. That's where I found my night creeper.

He was at the desk, riffling through the papers piled on it, looking frustrated. He was of slight build, and moved with a quick, nervous energy. A floppy hat and a dark shirt with the collar turned up hid his face.

Great, I thought. A "good ol' boy" who thinks he's The Shadow.

He looked around the room. There were bookshelves, packed solid with volumes that seemed to be mostly large paperbacks. A separate computer desk sat in the far corner. There were no other files or loose papers lying around. It looked like he was giving it up. He did look at the computer but decided against trying to get into any files.

I slipped around the house and made it just in time to see him leaving. He retraced his steps across the lawn, focusing on not being seen from the main building up the hill. He never even looked back. I was glad about that. If he had, I'd have been in the spotlight.

When he reached the line of trees I moved faster, hoping he would slow down, dodging the invisible obstacles of the undergrowth in the dark. Slipping through the line of trees, I crouched and closed my eyes, trying to speed their adjustment to the deeper darkness.

Suddenly I heard the whisper, from somewhere ahead of me. "I can see you, William Donley. I would kill you if there were not already plans for you. Do not attempt to follow me, if you want to find the girl alive. Now that we know you're here, you will be contacted."

I heard a rustling after that and then a silence that made the crickets and frogs sound loud went on until I felt safe to move.

This case just wasn't working out for me at all. I was practically a passive victim, letting everybody else have all the initiative. This was not the way I was used to operating. I was getting more than a little frustrated. Now I knew what he'd been looking for: evidence that I was here. In my eagerness to play superspy I'd given it to him before I was ready.

Well, if nothing else, I could talk to Omar. He still seemed to think I had something to contribute.

I turned and waited, watching, for several minutes before stepping back out onto the lawn. For a moment I considered returning to the director's house and trying to figure out if anything had been taken, but I'd have no idea what to look for. Besides, the way my skill was working, I'd probably be caught and accused if anything was missing.

The main building was brighter against the night. I looked up at the millions of stars and prayed, "God, I am way out of my depth here. As usual, I need Your help to even know what to do. I need to get Carmen safe. I need to minister to Omar. I need to give something to these students, and I need to confront this mercenary. Please help!"

Then I turned my steps back up the hill. It was time to mingle.

# Chapter 15

There was a fireplace, and logs were burning in it. The night wasn't that cold, but it still felt good. A semicircle of chairs faced the hearth. Omar was already there, sitting and staring into the flames.

Two girls were in a corner tuning guitars. One young man was sitting alone, reading. Two other guys were sitting with Omar.

Well, they weren't exactly "with" him. All three of them were staring mutely at the crumbling logs, apparently thinking profound thoughts.

I took the seat furthest from the flames, but still in the half-moon. When they looked up, I nodded and commenced my own staring.

They weren't going to let me get away with it.

One of them spoke up. "Uh...can I ask a question?"

"Of course."

"It's getting a little tiring, sitting and hearing all these people talking at us." The other guy tried to hush him, but he waved him off. "No offense, you know, but I'm kind of hoping there'll be a little more action this week."

"Action?"

He nodded, hopefully.

"What kind of action?" Omar said, as confused as I was.

"You know, like role-playing, witnessing practice, like that."

Yeah, like that. I could see steam pouring out of Omar's ears, so I figured I ought to be the one who responded. "Okay, practice. Hmm. That's very interesting. Yeah...yeah, I think we can do that."

"Great! Thanks! I'm going to enjoy this week."

Omar was staring even harder, trying not to glare at me. The kid had given me an idea. If "Ludlum" wasn't quite ready to make his move, we just might make it through this week.

I leaned over to him and whispered, "Let me take tomorrow. I think you'll be okay after that."

He considered for a moment, then nodded slightly, not taking his eyes off the burning logs. I leaned back and stared along with him, listening to the guitar music. The girls began singing softly, about God being higher than the mountains, deeper than the oceans and greater than heaven and earth.

After fifteen minutes or so I got up, stretched, looked at Omar--who was still staring--and left. Stepping outside, I walked briskly down the stairs and down the driveway from the main building to the road. I slipped past the rear of Buschmann's house. Across the road was the Elijah House.

Lights were still on, so they were still up. I made no attempt at being subtle. If they had guards on duty, I wanted them to know I had no hostile intent. I hoped they'd get the message, because I didn't have any handkerchiefs and they probably wouldn't believe a white flag anyway.

My suspicions were borne out. As I crossed the road and approached the small front porch, I heard a rustle in some nearby bushes and a voice said, "Halt!"

# Chapter 16

I froze, and waited for the rest of the drill.

It came quickly. "Who goes there?"

"A friend."

"State your name, friend."

"William Donley."

"State your business, William Donley."

"I wish to get acquainted and request a favor."

"Step up to the door please, Mr. Donley."

I did so, happy that I'd passed muster enough for the added "please" and heard him getting closer. "Take one step back, please."

I complied.

"Now, please lean forward, with your hands against the door. I am going to search you for weapons. I do not intend any harm or indignity toward you. Do you understand?"

"Sure. Go ahead. No problem."

The search was quick and expert, neglecting nothing. When it was over, he said, "You may stand up now. I'm sorry you had to experience that, but we've been threatened."

"Really? Not by the government, I hope."

"No, not yet. Mr. Lamphere can explain all that, if it's relevant."

"Does that mean I can go in?"

"Yes, sir. But please step to the left of the door as you enter and wait for me to announce you."

I followed instructions and found myself facing a crowded room. They were all men, seated in chairs, couches, and on the floor. One, a trim, gray-haired man, was standing with an open Bible in his hand. Everyone looked up as I opened the door and stepped aside.

A young, clean-cut guy stepped in behind me and said, "Excuse me, Mr. Lamphere. This is William Donley, and he says he has come to get acquainted and ask a favor."

Lamphere looked me up and down and nodded. "Get acquainted and ask a favor, eh? Okay. Well done, Termyson."

"Thank you, sir." With that, he about-faced and left.

"Mr. Donley, I look forward to making your acquaintance. I can't speak about the favor until I've heard it. Have a seat. We're almost finished."

I squatted on the floor and he went on. "As I was saying, gentlemen, the primary nature of the Christian's warfare is spiritual. Humans, no matter who they are or what they believe, are not the enemy.

"We have a double responsibility with this position we have taken. The secular press has branded us. They compare us with terrorists. Indeed, they confuse us with terrorists. Therefore, we must take every opportunity to demonstrate how wrong they are. Let us make sure that nothing inflammatory comes out of our mouths, and that we do not make issues appear where they are not.

"We are not only responsible for our families, against all comers...we are responsible to make sure that the accusations against us remain false; that there never is a grain of truth in them.

"Let's look at the Word of God for a moment."

Everyone but me had a Bible. I don't know why I didn't think I'd need one, but I was wishing I'd brought my little pocket Bible. I made a mental note to keep it with me from then on.

One of the young men next to me came to my rescue. He held his so I could look on and smiled at me. I shuffled a bit closer and leaned over his Book.

Lamphere was talking again. "Our passage tonight is in Luke's Gospel, chapter 3, and verse 14. Speaking of John the Baptist, Scripture says, 'Likewise the soldiers asked him, saying, "And what shall we do?" So, he said to them, "Do not intimidate (or shake down for money) anyone or accuse falsely and be content with your wages.'

"You see, John laid the foundations for two things here. First, there's a need for those who are sworn to protect us. We're living in a fallen world, so we have to be prepared to defend those who depend on us. We have to support those who are given that civil trust.

"Second, those who have that responsibility must have integrity, and must have compassion. We can't be hiring thugs to protect us, or putting up with them when they try to get into positions of trust.

"That must always be the difference between us and the kind of people the media say we are. We must have compassion and integrity. We must never use these skills to redress personal slights, or exact personal revenge. They are for defense, protection and help; not for satisfaction or advantage.

"And that's why I insist that everyone who joins this group have a valid, deep and personal relationship with the Lord Jesus Christ. I don't want any fringe crazies, or stereotyped religious paranoiacs. I want valid Christians in this group."

# Chapter 17

We sat down at a table in the kitchen, and someone said, "Excuse me, Mr. Donley?"

"Yes?"

"Do you drink coffee, sir?"

"Yes, indeed."

"How do you enjoy it?"

"Black."

Lamphere smiled. Soon there were two steaming mugs of coffee...both black... on the table between us.

He took a sip, set his mug down and said, "So, Mr. Donley. Now you have an advantage. You have become somewhat acquainted with us, but I still don't know anything about you."

I knew he figured I was in some way official. This wasn't going to be easy. "To start with, my being here has nothing to do with you."

"Can you verify that?"

"No. In fact, I'll have to insist that parts of this conversation will have never happened."

"You want me to lie?"

"Of course not. But refusing to repeat facts isn't the same as active deception... or is it?"

He shrugged. "It's a grey area. I can only say it depends. Tell you what, start with something that's not classified. Then I'll tell you if I even want to know the rest." I thought I was keeping a poker face, but he saw something there and chuckled. "We're not idiots, Mr. Donley. When my man got the drop on you outside, your response had 'pro' written all over it. You didn't lose your cool, and you calmly and slowly did what you were told. In this area, that makes you either mob or government. Your lack of discomfort during the talk, and other factors, told me you weren't a lawbreaker."

"Everybody's a lawbreaker."

"True enough. Now, tell me about yourself."

I started as far back as I could remember, giving him the fragmentary memories of my mother and her faith. I choked up a little describing my reaction to her death, but he just nodded sympathetically.

When I stopped, he summarized what I'd just said. "So, you were training to go to 'Nam, when your...er...ruthlessness, or mean streak, came to the attention of...someone."

I nodded.

"It sounds like you never made it to Vietnam."

"Right. Ironically, I was recruited out of the military."

"And now the classified part starts?"

I nodded again.

"I will assume then that the federal government found a way to put your anger to use. I probably don't even want to know the particulars. Since the Holy Spirit is bearing witness with my spirit that you are a child of God, I will also assume that you've been saved. Is that correct?"

"Yes, it is."

"Can you tell me about that part?"

"I can try."

"Okay. Give it a shot."

I gave him a version of Carmen's rescue that was so severely edited it barely made sense to my own ears. That didn't seem to faze him. He just sat, giving me his full attention.

When I stopped for air, he said, "It sounds like you were planning to resign from this, er, organization."

"Well, I hadn't made a decision yet, but that's definitely the direction I was going in."

"But something happened?"

I chuckled. "I was forced to take one more assignment, which turned into a confrontation with a nasty voodoo priest."

He grinned. "Who won?" he asked, knowing the answer.

I grinned back. "Jesus won."

A satisfied sigh escaped, then he got back down to business. "Are you on an assignment now?"

I shook my head. "No, but I'm smack in the middle of one. That guy I left alive snatched the girl again and wants me to come after her."

"He's here?"

"Very close, I think."

"And you're cooperating with your enemy?"

"I'm cooperating with my heart."

A nod of approval. "What can we do for you?"

"I met someone who was trying to find me earlier this evening. If you could just maintain the vigilance I saw here tonight and let me know if you see any characters creeping around, I'll be very grateful."

He stood up. "I think we can do a little better than that, Bill." He held out his right hand. "My first name is Alexander, as in Hamilton. I'd be obliged if you used it from now on."

I stood myself and shook the hand. "Thanks, Alexander. And you're right to call me Bill."

We stepped outside through the kitchen door. This time I could see one of the guards, standing next to a tree. If I hadn't been looking for him, he would have looked like a deformity of the trunk.

"I'm sorry to have interrupted your retreat," I said. "I hope I won't need the help. It's just that when I heard you were here, I couldn't help but wonder if there might be some support available."

"Well, there is. And now it's my turn to say the rest is classified."

"I deserved that."

"Not at all, but it's fun to say it. Feel free to join us again any time. We're not what you may have heard or read in the news."

"Thanks, I just might."

With that, I headed back across the street and up the hill. Though I was sure I was safe, I became aware of the little telltale sounds that I was being followed. When I got to the porch of the main building, one of rocking chairs shifted in the dark and Omar said, "Bill, don't you even want me to get saved?"

# *Chapter 18*

"Omar, I'm sorry. I...I don't know what to say. I didn't know you were that ready, I guess..."

"Nobody's ever ready for this. It's...it's the pits...it's terrible, Bill. I mean, I can handle murderers and traitors, double agents and saboteurs. I can handle firearms and unarmed combat. But, Bill, I'd rather fall into a swamp full of hungry 'gators than go through this."

I stepped closer and sat down in the rocker next to his, heavily. "I know exactly what you mean."

"I guess you do. But man, it's like, if God really is just, the only thing He can do with me is toss my carcass right into hell."

So that was still bugging him. I'd already given him everything I had about that, so I didn't know what to follow it with. "Mm-hmm."

"I hear the people talking about 'repent'. How do you repent, Bill? I'm as sorry as I can be. If I get much sorrier I'll be suicidal, but that's a sin too. There doesn't seem to be any escape for me."

"Well, I'm not too sure about the theological stuff, Omar. It didn't happen to me in my mind. I just had my heart broken over all the wasted years and knew how much God loved me to just wait through it all. I almost felt how much Jesus suffered to pay for those years. I took Jesus as my Lord, I guess they'd say. I didn't say a fancy prayer. I just kind of yelled at God; not in anger, but in desperation. I told Him to take my life and turn it into something He'd be happy with."

"Take my life...take my life..."

Just then a familiar voice startled us. "Sometimes a person can actually be too close to effectively lead his friend to Christ."

At least, it was familiar to me. Lamphere climbed the steps and joined us on the porch. "Forgive me for eavesdropping, gentlemen. It's a selfish and inconsiderate way to keep my skills honed, but I can't seem to help it."

Yielding to the inevitable, I said, "Omar, this is Alexander Lamphere, leader of the militia group down at the other guest house. Alexander, this is Brother Omar. At least, that's his working name."

Lamphere didn't wait for more of an explanation. "Omar, it sounds to me like you're under what the Bible calls conviction of sin. That's an uncomfortable place to be, but a very good one. It means you know that you need a Savior.

"Jesus Christ, the One who died painfully on a cross to pay for that sin, is that Savior whom you, and Bill, and I, so desperately need.

"Many years ago, I came to this place where you are and received Jesus Christ as my Lord and Savior. I can honestly say I've never regretted it, though some powerful people have tried to make me regret it. Your friend Bill here received Him only recently. Now, it appears, it's your turn. Would you like me to help you?"

That offer flashed me back to a room in a high-rise in Romania. Carmen and Olga. Why didn't I remember that sooner? I felt left out, almost resentful, like Lamphere had usurped my place in this.

They didn't even notice. Alex was leading Omar in a prayer very similar to Olga's. Common sense battered at my emotions and told me I had no right to the resentment. It didn't matter who prayed with Omar, as long as he got saved. Besides, this feeling wasn't...well, it wasn't Christian.

I began to really feel like a fifth wheel in this. Then, inside, I felt a gentle urge to slip away and get some much-needed rest. They were still sitting with their heads bowed. Omar might have been crying; I couldn't tell.

As quietly as possible, I stood up and stepped to the door. Lamphere looked up briefly. I waved to encourage him and stepped inside.

Once in the hall, fatigue caught up on me and I dragged myself down the hall, which now seemed unreasonably long, to my room.

I fell into bed, fully clothed, and was asleep immediately.

# Chapter 19

Once again, just like that night that felt so long ago, in Brooklyn, I was suddenly wide-awake. Something had crept under my consciousness and shaken my mind back to awareness. It was my inner, life-saving danger signal, telling me to get ready for something.

I maintained my position, though it was suddenly uncomfortable, willing whatever it was to happen again...

There! A sound, a scrape, from the window.

Outside. Someone trying to get in?

Possibly.

More likely, it was some hired hand trying to wake me up and make me believe he wanted to get in. This place wasn't locked up. Anybody could walk through the front door and right to my room if he was quiet enough. If you wanted to be sneaky, you could have come in earlier and left the exit door right by my room open. The window was unnecessary.

I had choices now. I could look for Omar, I could ignore the temptation and wait for a more advantageous time, or I could fall for the bait and get taken.

Without my own consent, my mind took me back to that night in Omar's shack by the lake on Great Inagua. I knew they would come for me, and I was supposed to let them take me.

I suddenly knew that whole Caribbean assignment had been a drill. It was a rehearsal for this. My involvement with Carmen had never ended, in God's sight. I was sent away from her for a season, just to be prepared for the reunion tonight.

It was time for another showdown.

There was another woman depending on me, like Chase in the Caribbean. This time it wasn't just a job; it wasn't my country requiring it of me. This time it was personal.

The scratch at the window came again, and I bolted up, as if just hearing it. The bush outside the window moved, ever so slightly, but enough. It was no breeze doing that.

I slipped out of the bed, put on my basic black outfit and stepped into the hall. I stopped long enough to splash my face in the bathroom, then went away from the nearest exit, which they'd be expecting me to use, to the stairs and down to the kitchen level. The hall down here was darker, but I knew there were other exits. I padded through the cafeteria to the doors that opened on the opposite side from my room and grabbed the knob.

The door hadn't been opened recently, so it took about a minute to open it with relative silence. Then I crept outside and crouched, not quite ready to be taken. After a few minutes I left the door open and moved, ever so slowly, to the shadows behind the building.

The graveled parking lot went right up to the service entrance. There was no way to be quiet unless I moved into the trees first.

I flattened out and did an army-crawl to the line of trees and crouched in the undergrowth, listening. The silence was total for a while. The little sounds that greeted me were all natural...at least, and they sounded right.

I crept from tree to tree, slowly, trying to avoid the bushes, vines and leaves that were everywhere.

After what felt like hours, I came all the way around and I could see my window. There he was, scratching the glass with something, huddled under the window between the wall and the bush.

And there were also two more of them in the trees behind me, trying to be quiet and thinking they were succeeding. I let them keep thinking it and listened to them as I kept my face forward.

I was braced for the rush of air that would precede a blow on the head, but it never came. Instead, a barrel dug into my ribs and a voice whispered. "Stay very still, Donley."

Quickly, and almost efficiently, I was patted down. A second voice, surprised, said, "He's clean!"

"Good. Easier all around. Okay, Donley, let's go. Turn slowly to your right and proceed to the hiking trail."

I complied and heard one of them hustling to the house. Soon there were three of them making noise behind me, two puffing. Finally, a new voice said, "Took him long enough."

The one who'd given me directions said, "Shut up," and everybody was quiet after that.

When I stepped out onto the hiking trail, he said, "To the right again," and I turned. The trail now went uphill, and soon we were all puffing as I maintained a healthy pace. At one point the path stopped and branched in two directions. My guide said, "Left," and we continued. After a minute or so of stumbling downhill I heard, "Stop," and halted. A flashlight shone to my right, and the voice said, "Find the stairs and climb down."

It was slow going, without being able to see ahead of me. I finally made it to the bottom and saw logs laid end to end on either side of the stairs. I stepped along it and came to a wooden bridge. "Keep going. All the way across." That told me it was a local guy. "Ludlum" had apparently hired some good-ole-boys for his dirty work.

Now we were in some kind of clearing, so I didn't know which way to go. I stepped off the bridge far enough away to let the others get off, then waited like a nice guy.

There was more tramping through the woods until we came to a place with some barbed wire. I was instructed to step through the opening two of them made and march through the field, which I did. Very carefully. This tramping went on until almost dawn when we came to a relic of a farmhouse. A ramshackle barn listed close by, but we headed for the house.

A single light was burning in what I guessed was supposed to be the living room. We had a visible objective. I didn't wait for instructions this time, just sauntered up to the front door and knocked like a traveling salesman.

# Chapter 20

That familiar, oily voice called out, "Come in, come in! I've been waiting for you, Mr. Donley."

I stepped inside, into a spacious room with a few sticks of furniture, and moved to the left to make room again for those behind me.

"Ian Ludlum, alias Vladimir Ninshka, I presume?" I said, pleasantly.

My gaze roamed the room. I saw him, grinning and posing in the center of the room, holding an automatic pistol casually at his side, pointed down.

Then I saw Carmen. Her eyes were wide, like when she'd heard me tell him to get saved. She saw me looking back and smiled.

I melted with a protective fierceness that transcended any other interests. Whatever else might happen, whoever might have to get hurt, Carmen would get out of this.

"Carmen," I said, "my name is Bill Donley."

"I know. He never stops saying it. He's obsessed with you."

"Well, he found me. He knew the right bait."

"You came for me," she breathed.

"That's right," I said, my voice surprisingly hoarse. "For you."

She blushed.

"Ludlum" caught the significance of the exchange and laughed. "How very touching, indeed. I am delighted to be the means of reuniting you two for this love scene. A tragic one, I'm afraid, but all the more touching for that."

I was still looking at Carmen. Her eyes asked the question, and I grinned in answer. She grinned back. "Not 'caught', just found," she said.

"There's a difference," I finished.

He caught the exchange and frowned momentarily, then brightened. "Oh, but I am not alone this time, in case you haven't noticed."

I looked around. Only two of my escorts had come in with me. I had no doubt there were others stationed around the property.

I had to concentrate on not relaxing. I didn't really respect this guy. He talked too much. That didn't mean I had a right to relax. I needed to stay sharp, and to keep him busy talking, thinking he had the upper hand...which, as far as I could tell, he really had.

"So, now you eliminate me in the middle of nowhere and spirit her out of the country, back to Romania, right?"

"Romania? Oh, no. I have no intention of traveling so far. You see, my real name is Jorge Padrega."

Carmen reacted to that, and he caught it.

"You're...you're..."

"Yes, I am Cuban. In fact, I am one of those who was originally assigned to your family, for your...uh...'protection'. You never saw me at home; I was assigned to your father's laboratory. I will take you back to the country you never should have left. And, eventually, 'invite' your father to return. 'Please come home. All is forgiven', like in those classified ads, no?"

"So you're not really a mercenary after all, are you?"

"No, no, no. That is a carefully cultivated fiction to help me get into countries that might not be open to foreign agents, even friendly ones. I am a true Marxist. I have even enjoyed some of Castro's speeches."

She folded her arms and glared at him.

I couldn't help it; I chuckled. "Looks like we're back to the old 'Smuggler's Ransom' gambit, huh?"

She locked his eyes and said, "You're boring."

"I am sorry you think so. I can change that very quickly. In a few moments you will hate me, but you will no longer think I am boring." He turned to me. "As for you, I must make sure of you this time. And I do not believe any helicopters will save you here."

The two who'd brought me here were on either side of me, both holding guns aimed at me. Padrega raised his, aimed at my head, and said, "This is ecstasy," and was about to pull the trigger when he heard something.

We all heard it.

Gunshots. Outside.

I shrugged. "They're always hunting something around here."

He held his hand up for the other two. "Watch them," he said, and moved to the front. He opened the door a crack, stuck his head out, and stepped back inside. Then he went to each of the other windows and looked out briefly.

When he came back to me, he was furious. "Did you let him bring an army with him?" he hissed at his helpers.

"I think I can do better than that," Lamphere had said.

They looked confused and frightened, so I volunteered. "No, I didn't bring them. They followed me."

The shots had been getting louder and more frequent. The action was getting closer.

Breaking glass shattered the silence in the room. Everyone turned to the window on my right that had just broken, only to be surprised by a huge form hurtling through the door.

The guard on my right tried to draw a bead, but a black fist smashed his jaw and he crumbled. Omar, going into a crouch, glared at me. "This is still my assignment, sucker!" he snarled.

As he turned toward Padrega, a shot rang out behind me and his left shoulder blossomed in a red splash.

I ducked, sending my right leg out behind me. The gunman doubled over and I sent my fist into his jaw, straightening him out and sending him to dreamland. His gun clattered across the floor and I lost my balance, coming up in a roll...

...with the muzzle of Padrega's gun a foot away from my nose.

His hand was shaking, his lips were twisting in a snarl of hate, and his eyes were black pools that almost looked drugged. "No-o..." he growled. "You don't get away this time...you don't..." His finger seemed to be in slow motion as it squeezed, pulling back the trigger...

It was point blank. There was nowhere to move without making him jerk back with that little bit of pressure that was all he needed now and send a bullet into my brain... I was really, truly out of options this time. Any second now...

The blast of a gunshot ripped through the room and a red hole appeared in the middle of his chest. He finished the squeeze, but the gun was pointing at the floor and it only singed my knees. As he crumbled, I looked around for the one who'd saved my life this time.

There stood Carmen, holding the forgotten gun that had skidded toward her when the gunman went down. Her face was a mask of shock, horror and determination. She clung to the hated weapon with both hands, glaring at Padrega and yet appalled at what she'd just done.

Realizing the crisis was past, she dropped the gun, very dangerously, on the floor and looked to me with mute appeal. After a moment, she blurted, "He was...he was going to..."

"It's okay," I said, getting up. "It's okay, Carmen. You saved my life. That's what's important. That's what matters."

"Oh, Bill..."

"Carmen..."

With the shots continuing outside, she wailed inarticulately and wrung her hands, tears streaming and her face twisted in an infantile frown.

I said, "Carmen, there's room for this in Scripture. You did well. I...I love you and want to make a future. You just made that possible."

I held out my arms and let my face ask the question.

She ran, almost knocking me over.

# Chapter 21

We only gave ourselves a moment before looking after Omar. He was in pain, but the wound was high enough that it missed all vital organs. He'd hurt for a while, but he'd be okay. We bound up the wound to stop the bleeding and cuddled on the floor, waiting for the action outside to stop.

She looked at me in a way I'd never seen before. "You came. Did the government send you?"

I shook my head. "I wasn't on assignment, though they wanted me to be here. I would have come even if they'd forbidden it."

Despite the shots outside, and the carnage inside, I kissed her. She responded, and I felt a fullness well up inside of my chest and fill up my throat like I'd never felt before. I almost started crying.

In about five minutes, silence reigned. Two minutes after that, the door opened an inch and a barrel came through.

"It's okay," I called. "The house is secure, but one friendly is down. We need medical help."

The door closed and opened again soon after that. Several men came in, Lamphere among them.

When he was satisfied that Omar was stable, he looked up. "Well, you sure know how to give an exciting retreat there, Bill!"

"My apologies. Retreats aren't supposed to be exciting, are they?"

"Not by definition. Now, is there someplace you can call so we're not all arrested and convicted? Some neighbors showed up with shotguns, so you'll want to make sure they're covered, also."

"Got a phone?"

He unsnapped a mobile phone from his belt and tossed it to me.

When I had assurance that a clean-up crew would be around soon, I tossed it back. "Speaking of retreats," I said, "I think it's past all our bedtimes."

He laughed. "Right you are, Bill. It's been a privilege to work with you!" He tipped his hat to Carmen and was out the door.

Carmen's lips found mine and we stayed like that, finding the words and caresses that said what we each needed to hear. Then we stumbled outside together. The sun was just rising. The sky overhead was still dark, though the eastern horizon was golden. Two jeeps were pulling into the yard.

We stood there, wrapped around each other, while the team deployed around us. Finally, I loosened the grip and looked at her, drinking her in.

Explanations would have to be made to the missionary school. Dr. Gonsalo would have to be called, and plans would have to be made. It was far from over, but I couldn't help stroking Carmen's cheek, wondering at God's grace and the wonder of this young woman and all she suddenly meant to me: the emotional healing, the salvation, the new beginning.

She spoke softly, saying, "Ecclesiastes says 'There is a time to kill, and a time to heal'."

I answered, just as softly. "The 'time to kill' is over...for both of us. Now it's time to heal."

235

# THE END

**You can find ALL our books up on our website at:**

*http://www.writers-exchange.com*

**All Steve's Books:**

*http://www.writers-exchange.com/Steve-Losee/*

**All our mysteries:**

*https://www.writers-exchange.com/category/genres/mystery-thrillers-suspense/*

# About the Author

Steve Losee has been a wordsmith of one kind or another for several decades. He has been a playwright, actor, advertising copywriter, journalist, columnist, preacher, teacher, counselor, newsletter writer, editor, book reviewer, poet, songwriter and fiction writer.

He now lives with his wife, Eira, in northern Pennsylvania. They're not far from their two grown children and three grandchildren. While busy with many creative projects designed to extend God's kingdom, Steve has plans for more fiction.

You can keep track of all his books with Writers Exchange on his author page:

http://www.writers-exchange.com/Steve-Losee/

If you enjoyed this author's book, then please place a review up at the site of purchase, and any social media sites you frequent!

**If you want to read more about books by this author, they are listed on the following pages...**

# One Last Hit

## {Mystery}

*Hard-boiled action with a soft-hearted hero!*

When a homeless drug addict is shot trying to confess something to Eric Thorne, nobody else seems to care very much. Eric starts to make his own inquiries and ends up mixing with underworld kingpins, federal agents, occultists, and several levels of human depravity. The trail leads through abandoned buildings, posh penthouses, street-level crime and high-level cover-ups. With an undercover narc, a beat cop, and a local pastor as his only allies, Eric digs into "Pegleg's" last days and uncovers a frighteningly familiar killer.

Publisher: http://www.writers-exchange.com/one-last-hit/

# To Die and Live A Bill Donley Novel

{Christian/Thriller/Romance}

*International intrigue and spiritual conflict collide!*

Turning to God always results in a major life change. For one man, it could mean the end of his life...

Bill Donley is a deep-cover, kill-or-be-killed counter-assassination agent in the days of the Cold War. When he accepts the gift of Christ's salvation in the middle of an assignment in the Balkans, he finds himself with two problems: His enemies refuse to believe he's been authentically converted, and his employers refuse to allow it!

From the USA Capital, Donley's adventures take him to Paris, Bucharest, New York City, the Bahamas, and finally to a deserted farm in the hills of Pennsylvania, where the life of the woman he loves hangs in the balance.

After successfully rescuing Bible smuggler Carmen Gonsalo, Bill is forced to take one more assignment, little knowing his archenemy intends to force a final confrontation.

Part 1 of this novel is the basis for the video "Smuggler's Ransom" by Noa/Rice Productions, available through Cloud Ten Pictures Inc.

Publisher: http://www.writers-exchange.com/to-die-and-live/

# The Genesis Threat

{Christian Thriller}

Embedded in an Alaskan glacier is evidence that would overturn more than a century of Western thinking.

The radical discovery sets off a deadly chain-reaction that stretches across the continent and changes the lives of several people, including a dissatisfied young Pennsylvanian man and a heartbroken Inuit woman. An entire culture is seduced by an illusion, but who can guess the extremes powerful people might go to in order to preserve the lie?

Publisher: http://www.writers-exchange.com/the-genesis-threat/

**You can find ALL our books up on our website at:**

*http://www.writers-exchange.com*

**All Steve's Books:**

*http://www.writers-exchange.com/Steve-Losee/*

**All our mysteries:**

*https://www.writers-exchange.com/category/genres/mystery-thrillers-suspense/*